The
Nine
Lives
of
Travis
Keating

The
Nine
Lives
of
Travis
Keating

Jill MacLean

Fitzhenry & Whiteside

Text copyright © 2008 by Jill MacLean
Published in Canada by Fitzhenry & Whiteside,
195 Allstate Parkway, Markham, Ontario L3R 4T8

Published in the United States by Fitzhenry & Whiteside,
311 Washington Street, Brighton, Massachusetts 02135

www.fitzhenry.ca   godwit@fitzhenry.ca

10 9 8 7 6 5 4 3 2 1

Library and Archives Canada Cataloguing in Publication

MacLean, Jill
The nine lives of Travis Keating / Jill MacLean.
Target audience: For ages 9-12.
ISBN 978-1-55455-104-0
I. Title.

PS8625.L4293N46 2008   jC813'.6   C2008-902322-6

**U.S. Publisher Cataloging-in-Publication Data
(Library of Congress Standards)**

MacLean, Jill.
The nine lives of Travis Keating / Jill MacLean.
[224] p. : cm.
Summary: Only some strange characters and a dangerous class bully seem to
take an interest in Travis when he moves to a small town in Newfoundland
after his mother's death. But the discovery of a colony of feral cats gives Travis
a chance to put aside his own grief and anger to care for them.
ISBN: 978-1-55455-104-0 (pbk.)
1. Feral cats — Fiction. 2. Cats — Fiction. I. Title.
[Fic] dc22 PZ7.M3643Ni 2008

Fitzhenry & Whiteside acknowledges with thanks the Canada Council for the Arts, and
the Ontario Arts Council for their support of our publishing program. We acknowledge
the financial support of the Government of Canada through the Book Publishing
Industry Development Program (BPIDP) for our publishing activities.

 Canada Council   Conseil des Arts
for the Arts   du Canada

 ONTARIO ARTS COUNCIL
CONSEIL DES ARTS DE L'ONTARIO

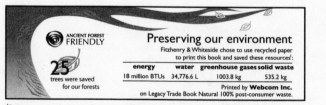

ANCIENT FOREST FRIENDLY

Preserving our environment

Fitzhenry & Whiteside chose to use recycled paper
to print this book and saved these resources[1]:

energy	water	greenhouse gases	solid waste
18 million BTUs	34,776.6 L	1003.8 kg	535.2 kg

25 trees were saved for our forests

Printed by **Webcom Inc.**
on Legacy Trade Book Natural 100% post-consumer waste.

 FSC

Recycled
Supporting responsible
use of forest resources

Cert no. SW-COC-002358
www.fsc.org
© 1996 Forest Stewardship Council

[1]Estimates were made using the Environmental Defense Paper Calculator.

Cover image courtesy of Tara Anderson
Printed in Canada

For Stuart,

who asked me to write him a book

One

Day 363...and Counting

Some Sunday nights, you should go to sleep and not wake up until Tuesday.

It's Monday. Monday morning, and the school bus has just stopped at the end of the driveway. Not a chance in the world it'll take me back to St. John's and 24 Willow Lane.

Bad enough changing schools. Worse doing it five weeks after school starts.

I tramp down the driveway. The wind's blowing off the sea, sharp and salty, tugging at my jacket, sneaking down my collar. A north wind, straight from Labrador.

When I climb on the bus, the driver says, "You're Travis Keating, right? Hi there. I'm Mr. Murphy. Sit anywhere you want."

I'm the first one on. I sit midway to the back, and we drive away. Next we pick up a girl he calls Prinny,

1

who has a straggly brown ponytail and sits at the front. A boy with ears that stick out gets on after her. His name's Hector and he sits at the front, too. Then we drive to Fiddlers Cove.

So there are only two kids my age in Ratchet. Total population: sixty-seven.

The first guy to get on in Fiddlers Cove is tall and skinny, with hair slick as molasses. Looks like he's in grade seven or eight. When Mr. Murphy says, "Hi, Hud," he doesn't say anything, just slouches down the aisle. He sees me and stops, holding the rail as the bus starts. His eyes are pale gray, like slob ice.

"You're in my seat," he says.

"There's lots of other seats."

"You deaf, squirt?" He reaches out, grabs me by the ear, and twists it. I'm not in the mood to take guff from anyone, even if he is twice my size. I punch out at him.

One of Dad's rules is Think Before You Act. Thing is, I usually act before I remember the rule.

"Hud, lay off," Mr. Murphy says. He's looking in the back mirror like he was expecting something like this to happen.

Sneering, Hud knuckles my cheek. "See ya at recess," he says and clomps to the back of the bus. My ear feels like he held a match to it.

Other kids get on, but no one sits near Hud. As the

bus fills up, a boy plunks down next to me and starts to talk. His name's Cole Sugden, and he's in grade six like me. Tells me how he plays hockey, left wing, but the rink isn't open yet because they're waiting for parts for the Zamboni.

Another downer. Hockey was how I planned to make new friends.

Cole sticks with me all the way to our homeroom. The teacher's name is Mrs. Dooks, and she looks like she just ate six sour apples.

She says, "This is Travis Keating, class. His father is the new doctor. Travis is from St. John's."

She says St. John's like it's the planet Krypton. A couple of kids snicker and my neck goes red. But the work seems okay, pretty much what I'm used to, and then it's recess. Cole's playing ball hockey with some other kids, so I go stand by the fence. Tomorrow I'll bring my old stick and keep it in my locker.

A gull swoops past. "*Klee, klee, kleeee,*" screaming into the wind like it lost its best buddy. I jam my hands in my pockets and scuff a hole in the ground with my sneaker. The first day's bound to be the worst.

I'm lining pebbles up in little rows with my toe when something makes me look up. Hud's sauntering toward me, stuffing his face with ripple chips. Although the wind's scudding around the schoolyard, his hair stays glued to his scalp. The teacher on yard duty has her back to us, over by the main door. All the kids go quiet, like the movie just started at Empire 12.

I click into stubborn mode. I'm scared, you bet I am, but I'm not going to let it show.

Hud stands so close that I have to crane my neck. "You from away?" he says.

"St. John's."

"Townie, eh?"

"What's the difference? I'm here now." For 363 more days, to be exact.

"We don't got much use for townies round here." He drops the empty bag, scrunching it into the dirt with his heel. "Specially runt-sized ones."

"My dad's six feet tall. I figure I'll catch up."

"Don't gimme lip."

"I'm not giving you anything."

"You talk funny, you know that?"

There's a reason I talk funny, although I'm not about to tell him why. He moves closer, crowding me into the fence so the wire mesh digs into my back. He stinks of sweat and stale cigarette smoke.

"Keep away from the other kids, okay?" he says. "I wouldn't want 'em to start talking fancy like you."

He steps on my toe with all his weight, grinding it into the ground. I make my face go tight, then I hide behind it—Funeral Face, that's what I call it.

His jacket's black. St. Fabien Furies embroidered on the pocket.

Hud turns around and says in a loud voice, "Don't none of you guys cozy up to the townie. You got that?"

The other kids sidle out of reach. He looks down at me. "And you better not blab to old Dooks. She and my ma are tight as crabs in a trap."

The bell rings, so shrill it makes me jump. Hud cuffs me on the side of the head, then walks away. I want to march out of the schoolyard straight to Dad's clinic and tell him we're hitting the highway nonstop to Willow Lane. Instead, I trail behind everyone else to the main door, where we line up to go inside. Everyone acts like I just rolled in dog poop.

Don't often have to use Funeral Face twice in one day.

Back home, Jasper Hines was the neighborhood bully, throwing kids' book bags in the ditch and stealing their lunch money. But me and my buddy Grady always hung out together, so he never bothered us much. Compared to Hud, Jasper was an amateur; he couldn't have turned a whole schoolyard against me.

On the bus that afternoon, I sit near the front. Hector and Prinny ignore me. So does Cole. As if I'm invisible. Or transparent, like water. Which we're seventy-five percent made of, but it's the other twenty-five percent that counts.

The only smile I get all day is from Mr. Murphy.

Or the next day, or the next.

At least Hud's leaving me alone, although every now and then when he sees me standing by myself at recess—all 100 percent of me—he gives a self-satisfied smirk.

Wish I could be Dad's size, just for five minutes. Then I'd be the one wearing the smirk.

Five minutes isn't much to ask.

Two

Day 360...Outcast

On Thursday, as we're waiting to pile on the bus after school, the kids are arguing about a place called Gulley Cove.

"It's haunted," Cole says. "Joe Baldwin got knocked off the wharf by a dead guy with slime dripping off his skull."

"Joe and six beers," Stevie Rideout says; he's a friend of Cole's.

"Yeah? I'd like to see you on that wharf after dark."

"The ghosts are there in the day," one of the girls says. "Sally saw one. Ran at her, wailing like a nor'easter. She won't never go back there."

"I bet it was old Abe Murphy," Cole says. "He's crabby enough to scare anyone away."

"He don't live in Gulley Cove."

"Used to fish there, back when."

Mr. Murphy levers the bus door open. Cole and Stevie get on first, still arguing. I sit near the front. I've got nothing to lose and I'm curious, so I say, "Prinny, you believe in ghosts?"

"No." She stares out the window.

"You, Hector?"

Hector grunts. A grunt's the most I've ever gotten out of him. My hands ball into fists. The kids in St. John's never treated me like I wasn't worth talking to. Then, to top it off, I remember the project Mrs. Dooks assigned last period. "A Portrait of My Family." Oh man, that sucks.

No way I'm telling her about Mum. That's what Funeral Face is about—keeping Mum buried. She's the reason I talk funny. She taught junior-high English, and she could really stress out about grammar.

Getting off the bus is like being let out of prison. I run up the driveway. The house Dad and I are living in is only one story and it's built on a rock. No basement, no trees. The barrens are behind it, on and on as far as you can see: scrub and granite and a few clumps of spruce. Nothing like our backyard on Willow Lane.

Never thought I'd miss a garden.

Dad built a tree house there when I turned seven. Grady and me kept an old wooden box in it for stashing the empty shot shells that littered the marsh every fall, and the black maggot casings we picked up near a dead raccoon in the woods off Linsey Street, where we weren't supposed to go. You could hear the maggots chomping away inside the raccoon, like it was whispering in its sleep.

I heaved those maggot casings out the window a year ago.

Inside the house, Rayleen's slumped in front of the TV in the living room, eating popcorn. "Did you wipe your feet, Travis?" she says without looking around to see if it's me.

For someone who watches the soaps like they're a zillion-dollar lottery, she doesn't miss much. "Forgot," I say and go back out to the porch.

I don't see why she has to be here when I get home from school. I'm eleven going on twelve; I don't need a sitter. Dad says she's not a sitter. His line is that she's the housekeeper, here to cook supper and keep the place clean.

I kick off my sneakers. "Where's Gulley Cove?"

That gets her attention. "Down past Abe Murphy's place. You're not to go there—one of your dad's rules. Rocks are slippery, sea's got a mean undertow, and the wharf's rotten as a winter apple. Off limits, you got that?"

"Yeah…I'm going for a bike ride."

"Put your books in your room and be back before dark," Rayleen says, chomping on the popcorn.

She's a Murphy. Nearly everyone in Ratchet is a Murphy or a Baldwin. Hector's a Baldwin and Prinny's a Murphy, although she's not Mr. Murphy the bus driver's kid or Abe Murphy's kid. Abe doesn't have any kids. He lives by himself.

Before I leave, I eat three caramel cookies, down a glass of Diet Coke, and rummage in my room for my fleece vest. Zipping it up, I go outside. The sea's throwing itself at the rocks like a kid having a tantrum. In case Rayleen's watching, I head left instead of right, pump up the hill, then turn around at the top and coast the whole way down, whizzing by our place and the six other houses.

I'm going to Gulley Cove.

I don't believe in ghosts.

❧

Abe Murphy's place is past the end of the pavement. When I come around the corner, I brake hard. A chill runs up the back of my spine. Two bikes are lying in the middle of the road. Hud Quinn and his sidekick, Marty Dunston, are standing near the picket fence watching Abe's brown dog bark itself hoarse as it lunges against its chain.

I dreamed about Hud last night. I know it was him.

Telephone poles in a row across an empty plain. I'm tied to one, trussed up so I can't move. A hangman's noose is looped around my neck. At first I think I'm alone on the plain. But then I hear shuffling in the dirt behind me, and slowly the noose starts tightening—I woke up scrabbling at my throat, gasping for air.

Hud bends over, picks up a rock, takes aim, and fires it at the dog. He hits it on the shoulder. The dog yips like a puppy.

Before I can think about what to do, an old man wearing dungarees and a red ball cap barrels around the corner of the house. He yanks the cap off, waving it in the air like he's shooing mosquitoes.

"You fellers get lost! Bother my dog again, I'll set her on you—you hear me?"

He bends over and looses the dog, who charges toward Hud and Marty. Snarling, she leaps at the fence.

Hud picks up his bike, taking his time. "You don't scare me none, Abe Murphy."

Marty picks up his bike, too. Which is when they catch sight of me. "It's the townie," Hud says. "Spying on us. I don't like him doing that, d'you, Marty?"

I whip the bike around and start pedaling back to Ratchet, bent low over the handlebars. Rocks twang against the spokes. A rut grabs the front wheel so I almost lose my balance.

They're stronger than me with bigger bikes, and they're gaining on me, so close I can hear one of them panting. I dart a look over my shoulder and pump the pedals like Lance Armstrong.

When I hit the pavement, the first house comes into sight. A woman's taking the wash off the clothesline, so I jam on the brakes right by her gate and slew to a halt.

Hud and Marty go sailing by, Hud shouting over his shoulder, "You got lucky, runt. Just you wait, though."

I'm gasping for breath, same as in the dream, my legs so shaky I can hardly stand up.

Slowly I begin to walk home. Pathetic to be this scared of a two-bit bully from a no-account fishing community. I never dreamed about Jasper Hines, not even after he stole the money I'd been saving to buy Mum a bottle of Oil of Olay for her birthday because she was complaining about being thirty-four years old, emphasis on *old*.

On our last English test, I spelled *humiliated* wrong. Put two l's in it. Hum-ill-iated's dead-on when it comes to me and Hud Quinn. He does make me feel ill.

At least the stones didn't chip the paint on my bike. Dad bought it for me new before we left St. John's.

It was his idea to move here. Not mine.

Three

Day 359...Ghosts

On Friday afternoon, Hud and Marty don't take the bus home because they're staying in St. Fabien to hang out at the mall. So I set out for Gulley Cove again.

Abe's dog barks at me like I'm out to steal the hens. "You can't catch me," I yell and skid down the steep hill past his place. The trail levels off, then slopes upward, following the cliffs. Two long bends, a dip into a hollow, then another climb, and I'm at the top. A couple of dead spruce trees, white like skeletons, point the way to Gulley Cove.

The sun's gone behind some clouds. At the bottom of the hill, a bunch of spruce trees are huddled along the shoreline. Parallel to the shore, there's an old wooden wharf on stilts; a long time ago by the looks of it, fishermen built five shacks in a row on the wharf for storing their gear. The trees look as though they're trying to shove everything into the sea: rickety old fish shacks, wharf, and stilts.

No boats because there aren't any fish. Rayleen told me the plant in St. Fabien closed down seven or eight years ago.

Gulley Cove doesn't look haunted. Just sad.

The slope's steep, so I rest my bike on some bushes and start walking, kicking at the stones. They roll down the hill, keeping me company.

The wind's banging a loose board against the wall of one of the shacks, and waves are slurping at the wharf. But as I get closer, I hear another noise. A thin, high wailing. It's the loneliest sound I ever heard in my whole life.

"*Aaaiiieeee…*"

I stop dead twenty feet from the first shack. I almost stop breathing.

"*Eeeeeooooowww…*"

My heart's banging around in my chest like a drummer on drugs. I don't believe in ghosts…do I?

"*Aaaaiiiieeeee…*"

Shriller this time, like someone being tormented. Maybe it's that dead guy with slime dripping down his skull and he'll chase me into the sea so I'll drown.

Something white streaks toward the middle shack. My feet unglue themselves, and I pound up the hill as if ten ghosts are after me. I don't see the rock until I trip over it.

My face is six inches from the road. A sharp stone's digging in my hand and my knees feel like they just hit concrete.

Granite, not concrete. A solid chunk of it, and it's torn two holes in my new cargo pants. Rubbing my hand against one knee to take away the sting, I stand up. That white streak was an awful small ghost.

Ghosts could come in different sizes. I guess. No reason why not, and even a little one's enough to frighten the pants off you. Rayleen told me how a bat flew down her chimney one night last summer. "Scared the living bejasus outta me."

She got that right.

Gulley Cove looks just like it did a few minutes ago. Deserted. Lonesome. Maybe I'll go home. Play *NHL* on XBox and forget I ever came here.

But if you can stick your hand through a ghost, you wouldn't think it could make a noise. Maybe a crazy old man—older than Abe, even—hides out in one of the shacks and doesn't want anyone bothering him.

What's crazy is me standing here gawking at a row of fish shacks. Chewing on my lip, I start down the slope again. The wailing could've been the wind through the gaps in the shack walls.

I wish Grady was with me.

"*Eeeeooooowww.*"

My scalp goes all weird. My fingers feel like they're holding lumps of ice. I keep walking toward the wharf, one foot in front of the other. Stones rattle on the landwash. The board bangs in the wind.

It's darker than it was ten minutes ago.

When my sneakers hit the wood floor of the wharf, they make a hollow sound. A shadow suddenly bursts through a hole in the wall of the middle shack. I yelp like Abe's dog. Then, as the shadow vanishes under the wharf, I sag against the nearest wall, shingles rough under my shoulders.

The shadow was gray. Not white.

It wasn't a ghost.

It was a cat.

Cat's howling—that's what the noise was. I'm some glad no one saw me charging up the slope like a cougar was after me.

Cats, regular cats, I can handle. But whose are they? Nobody lives here, or even comes here anymore.

"*Aaaaiiiieeeeooww…*"

This time I crouch down and creep alongside the second fish shack to the edge of the wharf. It's built high, with narrow tree trunks nailed together to make ladders for the fishermen to climb up from their boats. Maybe the cats used to belong to the fishermen.

I lie down on the worn boards and peer underneath

the wharf. From one of the joists, two yellow eyes with big black centers stare back at me. It's the gray cat, its bones shoving its fur out in sharp bumps. It bunches itself up, leaps from one ledge to the next, and disappears into the shadows under the wharf.

That makes two cats. One white and one gray.

Moving quietly, I edge along the wharf, stand on tiptoes, and look through the broken glass in the window of the middle shack.

Perched near the roof, a huge ginger cat hisses at me, drawing back its lips to show its teeth. Not very many teeth. Stained yellow. It's lost the tips of both ears, and a sore on one eye is leaking yellow pus. Gross. It hisses again and growls deep in its throat.

Looks as though it's using up its nine lives fast.

A scuffling comes from the next shack. One by one, I check them out, then search the rocks and trees. The list of cats goes like this: white, gray, big ginger, small ginger, white with black patches, black, and small gray. Seven cats. The black cat looks like she's going to have kittens, her belly heavy even though her shoulder blades stick out like knife points.

I should have gone home right after I tore my pants, then I'd never have seen the cats. I've got problems enough without adding them to the mix.

I rummage through the stuff in my pocket. Two dimes, a wad of Kleenex oily from my bicycle chain, my fancy whistle, and a pack of bubblegum. I unpeel the wrapper from the gum and start to chew. Grady gave me the whistle for my eleventh birthday last January. It makes different sounds depending on how you blow into it, and I carry it in my pocket all the time.

The sun's going down and the sea's turning black as it slides between the rocks. I run up the hill, wondering if the cats catch mice. Or birds. Or even rats.

I don't want a bunch of mangy cats. I want a dog. A big dog. But Dad says we can't have one.

You can't take a cat for a walk or play catch with it. Cats don't run to the door when you get home with their tails wagging and their tongues hanging out because they're happy to see you.

At the top of the hill I get on my bike, then ride back to the house as fast as I can. Can't seem to call it home yet. Home is our place in St. John's, which is rented to a family called the Bezansons. Snot-nosed Ralph Bezanson sleeps in my bedroom.

As usual, Rayleen's parked in front of the TV. The last soap of the day is just finishing, the music fading, then it's an ad selling toilet paper. She flicks the remote.

"I better get supper on the go," she says. "Fatten you up some—not enough flesh on you to bait a trout."

I'm not half as skinny as those cats.

They've been looking after themselves ever since the fishermen left.

They don't need me.

~~

Dad gets back from the clinic at six o'clock. His hair always looks like he's been out in a big wind, while his smile says he knows everything that's wrong with you and it won't take him any time to fix it.

That's a laugh.

When he tries to ruffle my hair, which is dark brown like his, I duck and we end up rolling around on the floor trading punches. He doesn't seem to notice that I aim to hurt. Rayleen shuffles around us in her pink shag slippers, dishing up ham and scalloped potatoes, my absolute favorite dinner. Once she's put the food on the table, she says good-bye and goes home to her family three doors down. Her kids are in high school.

The potatoes are cooked just right, with crispy cheese on top. Dad digs in.

"How was your day?"

"Why can't we get a dog, Dad?"

"I explained that to you already. You go to school on the bus, so you're gone all day. I drive to the clinic in St. Fabien, so I'm gone all day as well. There's no one—"

"—to let the dog out to pee or give it a run…yeah, yeah. You could hire Rayleen to come over at noon."

"Mind your manners," he says. "Rayleen doesn't like dogs. Or exercise."

"So find someone else."

"It's not feasible for us to have a dog. I don't want you bringing it up again." He stabs a chunk of ham. "I asked how your day was."

I checked out the ghosts at Gulley Cove and they turned into starving cats. "I aced a geography test and we're studying whales," I say, and that keeps us going until dessert. Chocolate fudge pudding.

"Did you go out after school?" Dad says.

"Went for a bike ride."

"Is your bike working okay?"

"It's a cool bike." Except I'd trade it in a minute to be riding my old beat-up bike with Grady and the other kids on Willow Lane.

Last August, Dad sat me down in the living room and told me he was feeling stifled in his job. *Stifled* was a new one on me, so I asked him what he meant.

"Choked. Suffocated. As though I can't breathe. But it's not just my job, Travis. I need to get away from here—the house, the neighborhood, the hospital, all the reminders of your mother."

Grown-ups are these big mysteries. You go along thinking you know what to expect, and then *wham,* it's like the skates have been knocked out from under you. Dad never talks about Mum, never even mentions her. Although I guess that's partly my fault.

Well, there's no *I guess* about it. No *partly*, either. Right after Mum died, Dad talked about her all the time, dragging her name in every chance he got. Like she was in the next room and he was just waiting for her to walk through the doorway.

Like he was trying to cover his tracks and pretend I could still depend on him.

All that changed the day of the Big Yell.

I was late for school that day because I couldn't find any clean socks; he'd forgotten to do the wash again. When I complained about the socks, he said, "Your mother always did the wash," and I erupted like a volcano and told him I was sick of hearing him talk about her, she was six feet under, and why did he keep acting like she wasn't. He went dead-white and quit talking about her altogether.

Except last August, around all this talk of *stifled*. But there was more to come. "I'm sick of suburbia, too," he said. "Remember where I was born? In an outport near Burgeo; no roads in or out. I don't want to go to a place that remote. But there's a position open on the northern peninsula, a clinic that looks after four or five fishing communities strung along the highway. We could live in one of them and go out in boats to see icebergs and whales."

"Forever?" I blurted.

"Let's say a year, for an experiment. We'll rent out our house here and rent a place there. That way, if either of us hates it, we can come back."

"What happens if you like it and I don't?"

"It could be the other way around, Travis."

"What happens though?"

"We come back here," Dad said.

"For sure?"

"For sure."

A year's not forever. So I agreed. Jeez, was that a big mistake. I didn't stop to think what it would be like without Grady or the guys on my hockey team, the St. John's Jets. Or even our own furniture. Snot-nosed Ralph isn't just sleeping in my room; he's sleeping in my bed.

I only thought how neat it would be to live in a place like Dad's outport and see whales up close. Not realizing they don't arrive until next July and the experiment begins in October.

Not realizing I'd feel like we've been here forever when it's been less than a week.

Four

Day 356...Brain vs. Brawn

In English class on Monday, I hand in "A Portrait of My Family" to Mrs. Dooks. Two-thirds of a portrait is what she's getting. I hate talking about Mum. Dad's a doctor, but he didn't fix Mum when she got sick. He let her die instead. End of story.

While I'm waiting for the bus after school, Buck Herbey, Cole, and Stevie are talking about Pete Corkum's Halloween party in Long Bight, and the scary videos they're going to watch. Buck, Cole, and Stevie hang out together; they're all on the St. Fabien Furies hockey team.

I haven't been invited to the party.

I bet Hector hasn't, either. Two losers. Him because he's chubby and hates gym, me because I'm the shortest kid in the room and Hud's made me as popular as a skunk at a dog show.

At Rawdon Elementary in St. John's, I wasn't a loser; the dorks and nerds might as well have been from the mainland for all I cared. I wasn't mean to them. I just ignored them.

Now it's your turn to be ignored, this voice says in my head. *Let's see how you like it.*

After I get home, I ride my bike to Baldwin's General Store to buy licorice cigars. First person I see is Prinny Murphy in the parking lot outside the store, face-to-face with a woman in a dirty blue sweat suit who's swaying on her feet like she was on the Tilt-A-Whirl. They're not bothering to keep their voices down.

"You can't hitch a ride to St. Fabien," Prinny says. "It's time to go home, Ma."

"Who says?"

"I do. You gotta cook supper."

"Baldwin's is clean out of rum. I gotta get to the liquor store before it closes."

"It don't close till ten."

I lean my bike against the store. Prinny's mother smells like Uncle George when he hits the bottle. Prinny gives me a dirty look.

"You got nothing better to do than gawk at us?"

"I've got as much right to be here as you."

Prinny grabs her mother's elbow. "C'mon!"

"There's Wilky Baldwin. He'll gimme a ride."

Prinny's mother waves her hand. A Ford half-ton pulls up and she staggers over to it, giggling like a girl in grade seven. The truck drives off with her in the passenger seat. Prinny stares after it, her shoulders hunched. Then she walks past me as if I'm not even there.

She's another loser.

Maybe she should start cooking her own meals.

Inside the store, the candy and chips are in the same aisle as pet supplies. Dog chow is stacked in big bags, with a heap of dried-up pigs' ears next to the Milk-Bones.

I can't have a dog. No use even thinking about it.

Cat food's farther down the aisle. One box has a picture of a ginger kitten washing its paws. On another box, a fluffy white cat's eating out of a fancy bowl. No sign of its ribs.

The only time I've ever been really hungry was when Dad sent me to bed without any supper because I stole five quarters off his desk to buy an Aero bar at the Quik-Way.

Rule #1: No Stealing.

Once I've paid for the licorice, I head home. But instead of going indoors to play *Ultimate Spider-Man*, I ride past the house, taking the corners slow in case Hud's around.

Abe Murphy's in his field, leading a brown and white cow to the barn. He stops and stares at me, and the cow turns her head too, mooing like she's got a bellyache. The dog starts barking. Abe yells, "Shut up, Lucy!"

Lucy shuts up. I keep going. I can feel him watching me until I'm out of sight over the hill.

On the ocean side, the track's lined with clumps of skimpy spruce trees beat up by wind and salt. Rayleen calls this "tuckamore." On the other side are the barrens, where the little shrubs have all turned red, as if they're on fire. You never know what you're going to find on the barrens. The fourth morning we were here, Dad and I saw two caribou behind our place; when they ran away, they bounded like they had springs in their heels.

At the top of the last hill down to Gulley Cove, I skid to a stop. Right away I recognize the two bikes leaning against a spruce tree. On high alert, I wheel in a sharp circle. No way I'm sticking around if Hud's at the cove.

I dreamed again last night...*water dripping down the walls of a deep pit. The corners full of shadows and no way to climb out. Then a hail of dirt comes at me. As I throw up my hands to protect my head, the dirt's already piling up around my legs, trapping me so I can't move. I'm being buried alive...*

Two days before the service, I overheard Dad talking about Mum to the funeral director, insisting on a closed coffin, as near as yelling that she hardly ever wore makeup when she was alive, and no one was going to plaster it on her face now that she was dead.

Don't get me wrong, I never thought they'd buried her alive—she *was* dead inside that coffin. But back then, the funeral was like the worst dream I'd ever had, and any minute I expected to wake up because your mother doesn't just up and die on you.

Okay, okay, so I'm still stuck in that dream and it's called reality. But I'm not stuck in last night's dream; I'm at the top of the cliffs instead, the sea wind chasing itself through the shrubs. I dump my bike on the ground, duck behind the spruce tree, and peer down at the cove. Hud Quinn and Marty Dunston are throwing stones at the wharf, watching them bounce into the water.

The big gray cat hitches itself over the edge of the wharf and scurries between two of the shacks. Hud and Marty race after it, firing rocks and shouting. A rock hits its back leg. The cat staggers and almost falls. But then it gets its balance and streaks toward the boulders, disappearing into the bushes.

I open my mouth to yell at Hud. Then I close it. I can't take on Hud, let alone the two of them.

I back up, so angry it's like the volcano is inside me again, boiling and bubbling and about to spew. I've got to act fast and I've got to use my brains. That's what I do playing hockey. When you're the smallest kid on the team, you either use your brains or you're toast.

First I hide my bike in the tuckamore, making sure it doesn't show from the road. Then I leave the track and creep down the hill, ducking behind the boulders and spruce trees, watching every step so I don't make a noise.

Hud's shouting again. I risk raising my head and see the big ginger cat take a flying leap into the safety of the woods. A rock thuds against the trunk of a birch tree.

Near the bottom of the hill, I luck onto a trail and end up in the trees behind Marty and Hud. They're zapping stones against the nearest shack. "Didja see that ginger cat?" Hud says. "We sure hustled his butt."

"You zinged the gray one."

"Yeah...let's case the fish shacks. Maybe there's more cats inside."

What if it's the black cat, the one that's pregnant? She probably can't run as fast as the others.

I'm scrabbling for a good-sized rock to fire up the hill in the hopes it'll distract them when my wrist brushes against my pocket. The whistle, the fancy one Grady gave me. I pull it out, take a breath, and blow into it, not too hard. It wails, lonely and sad.

Marty goes still. "*What's that?*"

"Dunno."

I blow again—harder, then softer, again and again, so it sounds like someone crying and moaning.

"It's the ghosts!" Hud cries. "I'm outta here."

Staying hunched down, I blow again. Marty and Hud dash along the wharf and up the hill like it's track and field day. At the top, they grab their bikes and pedal out of sight.

I give a victory *whoop*, my arms up high as though I'm holding the Stanley Cup.

That was better than the final game of the playoffs last April, when I ducked under the defenseman's arm and whipped the puck in the five-hole. I'm used to winning in hockey. But it's awesome to outsmart guys like Hud and Marty. They won't be in a hurry to visit Gulley Cove again.

Right this minute, I'm not one bit scared of them.

Although I poke around in the trees, the cats stay hidden. But when I go in the end shack, the black cat's sitting way up in the rafters, her fur all puffed up, her eyes big as marbles. If Hud and Marty had come in here, she'd have been trapped.

I stare at her, chewing my lip.

Five

Day 356...$7.82

Back at the house, Rayleen's vacuuming Dad's bedroom. I poke my head around the door. "I'm going to the store."

"Don't take your bike. It's too dark."

In my room, my hockey trophies are lined up on the shelf. A poster of Sidney Crosby hangs on the wall, and Mum's picture sits on the dresser—the one where she was perched on a ladder pruning the apple tree, sunlight all tangled in her hair. When she hugged me, she smelled of lilac soap. *My duck,* she'd call me, *my duckie,* which I really liked, although luckily she never called me that in front of my friends. When she was mad, it was *Travis Roland Keating,* like the time she caught me taking apart Dad's stethoscope to see how it worked; or the day I drank what was left in Uncle

George's silver flask when he was snoring on the couch, and I didn't make it to the can before I heaved.

My money's under the bed in the cab of my old John Deere tractor; I'm saving for a remote-control car. If I'm only buying licorice cigars, fifty cents is enough.

I roll the two quarters around in my palm. Because Grady's whistle was in my pocket today, the black cat didn't get hurt. But she's still hungry and she's still going to have kittens. I cram some loonies and toonies in the pocket of my jeans.

The store's crowded. Two kinds of cat food are on the shelf, the dry, crunchy kind in boxes, and little cans of beef stew. The puddles in our driveway have frozen a couple of times already, so likely the canned stuff would freeze. I pick up three boxes of dry food.

When I turn around, Hector Baldwin's standing there, tearing open a bag of Cheezies. Mr. Baldwin, who owns the store, is his uncle. "Hi, Hector," I say. Hector grunts.

I put the cat food down by the cash register. Mr. Baldwin smiles at me. His teeth are yellow like the big ginger cat's, but it's from chewing tobacco and spitting into an old Campbell's Soup can he keeps under the counter. While Dad's never made a rule about chewing tobacco, I'm not that keen to try.

"Didn't know you had cats, Travis," Mr. Baldwin says and slips me a green jawbreaker. Even though he's always been nice to me, telling the truth's not on.

"It's for a friend," I mumble.

Then I remember Hector, who knows I don't have any friends, not at school, on the bus, or in Ratchet. I never spent so much time on my own in my whole life—makes me lonesome as a coyote on an ice floe.

"That'll be $7.82, tax included," Mr. Baldwin says. "How's your dad? Keeping busy, I hear."

"He's fine."

"You a hockey player by any chance?"

"I play right wing."

"The St. Fabien Furies could do with some new blood—lowest scorers in the league last year." He spits into the can with a little pinging sound, then counts out the change and puts the three boxes in a plastic bag. "Too bad they can't hurry up the parts for the Zamboni."

I pick up the bag and thank him for the candy. I'm really good at scoring goals. When those numbers start flashing up on the board, the guys on the team won't care where I come from or how I talk.

Maybe then I won't have to sit at the front of the bus with Prinny and Hector.

Six

Day 355...Meltdown

When I drive past Abe Murphy's place the next day, he's sitting on his front steps, whittling a chunk of wood with a penknife. Lucy runs for the fence, barking.

To save time, I coast down the last hill to Gulley Cove. Three cats leap from the rocks, where they've been sunning themselves, and disappear into the trees. Then everything's still again. Except for the sea, which is never still.

I leave my bike at the bottom of the hill and take a box of cat food and a bottle of water out of my pack, along with some plastic bowls I stole from the cupboard this morning.

Rule #1's taking a beating.

The bowls should go inside the shacks in case it rains. The first shack's got a rusty padlock on the door with the window boarded shut. The second one's the same, although the padlock's newer. I walk toward the middle shack, the one with the broken window.

"*Eeeeeooooowww…*"

My scalp goes creepy, even though I don't believe in ghosts. The ginger cat's inside glaring at me as if I'm here to shoot it, not feed it. Its eye looks worse, glued tight shut.

"You got attitude," I say. "I bet you're a guy cat. Did people just go away and leave you? Like you weren't important?"

He hisses, lashing his tail. He's crouched down on the floor and looks bigger than he really is, so right away I decide to call him Felix, after Felix "the Cat" Potvin, the famous NHL goalie that Dad raves about.

The window's too high for me to climb in, the broken glass shining like Abe Murphy's penknife. But there's a small gap in the boards only a couple of feet away from Felix. I go round the other side, fill a plastic bowl with the cat food, kneel down, and shove it through the hole.

"*Ow!*" As I jerk my hand back, some of the food spills out of the bowl. Three claw marks run from my wrist to my thumb.

Felix yowls on the other side of the wall.

I'm trying to help and I'm the one who's bleeding?

One of the Kleenexes in my pocket isn't too oily,

so I wrap my thumb in it, watching the blood soak through. To take my mind off the pain, I edge over the rotten boards in the wharf toward the next shack. This one's easy. Part of one wall's gone and the bottom of the door looks like someone kicked it in. I fill two dishes to the brim with food and one with water, and put them in the corner near a stinky coil of rope.

The last shack's in even worse shape, the door hanging on its hinges, the roof sagging. The last two bowls go in there, one with food, the other with water. I'm backing out onto the wharf when the white cat suddenly races from behind the door right between my feet. I lurch backward.

My heel breaks through the boards.

The empty water bottle goes flying. I'm falling, flailing at the air, grabbing for the edge of the wharf. One shoulder bangs against the ladder. My wrist *thunks* into a crossbar, the wood slimy with kelp. Then I'm waist-deep in the sea.

The water's ice-cold, the shock making me yelp. Staggering, I wrap my hand around the crossbar. A wave sloshes up my chest, thrusts me against the wood, then drags me back.

My legs are turning numb. So are my fingers.

Another wave pitches me around like I'm no bigger than a jellyfish. Then I lose my grip and the sea's got me, doing its best to pull me under.

My feet scrabble for a hold on the bottom. But the rocks are smooth and slippery, and the seaweed is wrapping itself around my knees like eels. I thrash the surface of the waves, splashing and slapping, desperate to keep my head above water.

Do something or you're dead meat.

Wedging one foot between two rocks, I lunge for the crossbar again. My fingers wrap themselves around the wet wood, the muscles in my arm quivering with strain. The next wave surges toward the wharf, letting me push off from the bottom and jam one foot in the angle of the bars. My free hand grasps the next cross-bar, then my other leg's out of the water, my sneaker finding a foothold.

Slowly I haul myself up, grunting like Hector. When I finally crawl onto the wharf, I fall face down, dig my nails into the wood, and hang on. The wind slices through my wet clothes, making me shiver and shake. Doesn't matter that I'm an okay swimmer; anyone could drown in water that cold.

I gotta get out of the wind. Or freeze to death.

I get up on my knees, head hanging down, my bones aching like I'm as old as Abe. Then I stagger to my feet. Water squelches in my sneakers. Bracing myself against the wall of the end shack, I edge past the jagged hole in the boards and stumble toward the next shack.

It's empty. I shuffle to the far corner, drop to the floor, and curl up in a ball against the coil of rope. Even though I'm out of the wind, and even though I'm hugging myself tight, I can't stop shuddering. My teeth are clattering, heels drumming on the floor, and all I want is for Mum to tell me everything's going to be okay.

The first sob bursts out, then the second, and suddenly I'm howling like a coyote, dripping tears and seawater onto the old wooden boards. A memory that I buried along with Mum surges through me: the way she hugged me in the hospital on the very last day, hugged me like she never wanted to let go, like she'd saved every bit of her strength for it, her bones digging into me, her eyes so full of pain that I had to look away.

In the end, I run out of tears. My eyes are burning, the rest of me stone-cold. As though it belongs to someone else, I realize my thumb's throbbing from the claw marks. I better pull myself together. Start for home. It'll be dark soon. I lift my head and a black streak whips through the gap by the door.

The black cat was watching me. Watching over me.

If I start crying again, I'll be here all night.

I swipe my hands over my face. My jeans are soaked and so's my jacket. Oh man, this'll freak Rayleen out. But the whistle's still in my pocket and the pain in my thumb's nothing major.

Once I'm on my feet, I stamp them up and down to get the circulation moving, and bang my arms around my chest. Outside, the wind's still brutal. I sling my pack on my back, pick up my bike, push it up the hill, and ride home as fast as I can.

On the front step, shivering again, I take off my sneakers and wring out my socks. Then I creep into the porch. Luck's with me; it's the last five minutes of Rayleen's favorite show. I whip down the hall, get some dry track pants in my bedroom and head for the back porch. There's goose bumps up and down my legs, and my toes are pale blue.

I just made my last trip to Gulley Cove. Cats or no cats.

The black cat wasn't watching over me. She was in the shack because she smelled food.

❧

When we moved here, Dad taught me how to use the washer. In go the torn cargo pants, the wet jacket, jeans, and socks, and a bunch of T-shirts for camouflage. My sneakers get propped on the baseboard heater. Then I close the door and go to the bathroom.

My eyes are puffy, as though I've got allergies, and I feel hollow inside. The claw marks look gross. After washing them with soap, I cover them with the biggest plastic bandage in the box.

Rayleen's in the kitchen with the radio blaring. "You start a wash?"

Dad's dead-set against lots of things. No Lying being Rule #2, close on the heels of No Stealing. "I was skipping rocks," I say, "and didn't see a wave coming. What's for supper?"

"Not many rocks round here flat enough to skip."

She doesn't look half as sleepy holding a paring knife as she does in front of the TV.

"Meatloaf?" I say.

"Did your sneakers get wet? Put them in an old pillowslip and throw them in the dryer on low. What happened to your thumb?"

"Scraped it on the rocks. I'll go dry the sneakers."

Lying gets easier the more you do it.

Later on, Dad asks about my thumb. Except he's sitting across from me at the table, not busy peeling potatoes and singing along with Dolly Parton.

"Scraped it on some rocks."

"Is there dirt in it? Maybe I should take a look."

"It's okay—I made ninety-eight in a French quiz."

"Good for you. Where were the rocks?"

I mix corn and potatoes with my fork. "Up by Abe Murphy's."

"I don't want you going any farther than his place, Travis. That's a rule. Anyway, it won't be long before you'll have to put your bike away; winter comes early around here."

A year and a half ago, when Mum got sick, Dad started making rules. He hasn't stopped since. I said to him one day, "Why don't you make a rule not to make any more rules?" But he didn't think it was funny. Most of the time he acts like he's scared to let me out of his sight. I don't care what he says about Rayleen scrubbing the kitchen floor; he hired her to keep an eye on me.

"Are we going to buy a snowmobile soon?" I say. That was part of the deal in moving here. Grady's dad has one and sometimes we borrowed it.

"I'm at the clinic this Saturday, so I thought we could go to St. Fabien the following weekend. One thing about being this far north, there should be lots of snow."

"Will we get an Arctic Cat or a Ski-Doo?"

"I picked up some brochures on my way home. We could check them out after the dishes are done."

It's my job to do the dishes, pots and pans and all; that's how I earn my allowance. Buying the cat food made a big dent in my savings. Maybe Mr. Baldwin will give me a refund for the two boxes I didn't open.

I'll take them back tomorrow.

❧

That night I dream about Hud drowning me in the sea, and about sharks with cat faces, which chase me into a cave. My mum's in the cave. She's swimming away from me, then she turns into a rainbow trout that flicks its tail and vanishes.

When I wake up the next morning, the dream's still hanging around. I've had lots of practice not thinking about Mum. But the cats aren't as easy. Felix, who scratched me. The white cat, trapped behind the door in the end shack. The black cat, hungry, bony, bolting the instant I moved.

I'll take the cat food back to the store after school. Gulley Cove's no place for me. Too many rules flying out the window, and yesterday I came so close to drowning it still gives me the shakes thinking about it.

It's wet and windy by the time Mr. Murphy drops me off, the rain mixed with little ice pellets, so I stay home and play *Need For Speed* in my room.

I'm not going anywhere. I never want to be cold again.

Seven

Day 353...Left or Right

Thursday afternoon's sunny. As I shove the boxes in my backpack, the fluffy white cat in the picture stares up at me, fat and clean and healthy.

All the way down the driveway, an argument's going on in my head. Take the boxes back and forget about the cats. Enough crap's going on at school without adding Gulley Cove to the mix. Or the other side of the argument—keep feeding them. I can make their lives better even if mine's gone down the tubes.

When I reach the road, I look both ways. Left to the store. Right to Gulley Cove.

The sea's a deeper blue than the sky, and I wonder why it's never the other way around. I should ask Dad; he knows a lot of off-the-wall stuff, the kind of things you never learn in school.

I hated being hungry that night Dad made me miss

supper. All I could think about was hot fudge sundaes; and the next morning I dumped half a box of Cheerios in my bowl. Looks like the cats have been hungry for months, breakfast being whatever they can catch.

Besides—a real bonus—the cove's probably a Hud-free zone now, because of the "ghost" he heard.

What's a few broken rules anyway?

I turn right, toward Abe's place and Gulley Cove.

Abe's working on his old truck, and he straightens up as I go past. Lucy barks. All the way to the cove, I don't have a clue if I've made the right choice.

Felix isn't in the middle shack. But the dish is empty and so's the floor where the food spilled when he scratched me. The other dishes are empty, too.

That's a lot of cat food.

Maybe rats are eating the food. Or dogs. At Baldwin's Store they were talking about a pack of dogs running the barrens, chasing caribou. You're supposed to keep your dogs fenced or tied up, but not everyone does.

After filling all the dishes with food and water, I back away from the wharf into the trees, crouch down low, and wait.

Pretty soon the black cat comes sneaking out from between two rocks, her belly just about touching the ground. The wind rattles a shingle on the roof and she freezes. Then she creeps across the wharf and goes into the fourth shack. Through the gaps in the wall, I can hear her crunching the cat food.

Makes me feel warm inside.

Next, Felix hauls himself up from below the wharf and marches into the middle shack, what's left of his ears twitching. His eye looks the same as yesterday. Shut.

He needs a vet.

I can't afford a vet. Not on eight bucks a week.

Although the light's fading fast and my feet are cold, I stay put for another ten minutes. I catch a glimpse of the white cat and the one with black patches—Ghost and Patches, that's what I'll call them. It didn't take any of the cats long to find the food.

Now that I've fed them twice, I can't stop. That would be worse than not starting at all.

Tomorrow I could try coaxing them nearer with a dish of food. Taming them, so they'll trust me. But right now I have to hurry home or Rayleen'll be on my case. "See you guys tomorrow," I say, and I know it's a promise I've got to keep even though I wanted a dog and not a bunch of half-wild cats.

Deep down I'm almost sure taming them's not going to happen overnight.

Eight

Day 352...Blackie the Brave

Every Friday, school's let out half an hour early. I get to Gulley Cove in record time, hide my bike at the top of the hill just to be safe, and run down to the wharf. I spent recess thinking of more cat names, Step One in the plan to tame them. Step Two is to get near them.

I fill the bowls, moving slow and talking real easy, as if I'm talking to myself. "Hey there, Felix. How's your eye today? Blackie, you planning to have those kittens soon? Where are you hiding, Ghost? And Rocky, you're the same color as the rocks; it'd be easy to miss you. Hope your leg's okay where Hud hit you with the stone."

If I was Rocky, I'd run for cover if a kid came anywhere near the fish shacks. "Supposed to rain hard on Sunday," I say, "but my dad's at the clinic all day tomorrow, so I can come here then."

I don't feel one bit foolish. Makes sense to me that they'll get used to my voice along with the sound of the dry food hitting the bowl. I'm in the fourth shack when a face pokes through the hole in the wall. I pour more food into the bowl and keep talking. "That you, Blackie? You don't look so good."

She's hungry. And she's scared. It's a toss-up which will win. I slide the bowl nearer the door, not looking at her. "No need to be frightened. My name's not Hud...wish I could've wiped the floor with him."

I ease back into the corner and sit still. Blackie skulks toward the bowl, head low and ears back. Even her whiskers are quivering. Then she picks up a piece of food and starts chewing. "You're a brave cat to come this close," I whisper. "D'you think Rocky and Ghost will get up the nerve to eat in here, too? Or is it because you're extra desperate?"

For a while I just listen to Blackie crunching the food. It's a great sound. Satisfying. Like when your skates cut into the ice clean and sharp, or when the puck hits the frame at the back of the net. *Thwack.*

I turn my head slowly until I'm looking right at her. Her coat's raggedy and stiff, and I can count six of her ribs. Then Ghost pokes his head around the broken boards. When Blackie growls at him, he backs out in a hurry.

All this time, the waves have been playing tag under the wharf.

After a while, Blackie sits back. She starts to wash herself, one paw first, looking at the paw like it's not something she's washed for a good while. She rubs it behind one ear and then the other.

My knees are cramped, my ear itches, and the smell of old bait's stuck up my nose. Last summer, Dad told me about these monks in Tibet who sit still for hours. It's called meditating. So that's one thing I know I don't want to do when I grow up.

I'm not into scaring Blackie, though, so I stare at those dirty floorboards as if I'm an apprentice monk. She washes both paws, both ears, her forehead, her chin, and her chest. That's when Felix sticks his big head through the door.

Blackie hisses. But it's a halfhearted hiss. She gets up and slinks out between two boards as Felix plods in. He might be one-eyed but he's the boss.

"Hi there, Felix. How're you—"

He does an about-face and he's gone.

"I didn't mean to scare you," I say to the empty shack and stretch out my legs one by one.

Even though he's run away, I still feel good. The best I've felt since we moved to Ratchet.

Neat to know you've made the right choice.

Nine

Day 351...Ambush

Saturday's the last day of October. Halloween. If I was back in St. John's, Grady and me would be talking about our costumes and which houses dole out the best treats. We always went out together, carrying pillowslips and green light-sticks. I wish I'd quit missing him. Him and the St. John's Jets.

Then there's Gulley Cove. I hope no one goes out there tonight, partying, or on a dare because of the ghosts.

Nothing like adding seven cats to my list of worries.

Dad's already left for the clinic; he won't get home until five. Rayleen makes waffles. I'm in too much of a hurry to drip little ponds of syrup up and down the rows like I usually do. "I'm gonna pack a lunch and go out back of Abe's place to look for caribou," I tell her. "I'll stay in sight of the houses."

She gives me a look that says *I brought up three boys and you can't fool me.* "Wear a jacket and gloves," she says. But then she offers to make my lunch, so that's cool.

I shove water and a box of cat food in my pack, along with the hammer and nails I found in the back porch, and set off for Gulley Cove.

There's wash on the line again at the last house before Abe's. Then the pavement ends. I'm tooling along, weaving through the potholes, not thinking about much of anything, when all of a sudden Hud comes around the corner on his bike. He sees me and stops in the middle of the road, a big smile on his face.

Too late to turn around.

As if I'm at the rink on skates, I head right for him. But at the last minute I dart around his back wheel and belt down the road toward Abe's.

I should've remembered Hud's a hockey player, too. He recovers fast, following me until he's so close I can hear the gravel scrunching under his tires. His bike comes level with mine. As he grabs at my handlebars, I brake hard. His tires slew in the dirt but he doesn't let go. I fall off, the bike landing on top of me.

He hauls the bike off, throwing it in the ditch, and rips the pack off my back. "Gotcha," he says, and shoves me facedown in the dirt. Then he sits on me, all his weight on my ribcage.

Rocks dig into my nose and I'm eating grit. He bounces up and down, driving the air out of my lungs. Panic closes my throat. I can't move my arms, can't kick him, can't even breathe. Is he ever going to let go?

Buried alive...

A dog starts barking, loud and excited. Someone shouts, "You get off him else I'll fill your butt with more lead than a sunk goose!"

Hud slides off me and stands up. I turn my head to one side and take a shallow breath. Then another. I'm trying not to cry. Too humiliating. One *l*.

"You wouldn't dare shoot me, Abe Murphy," Hud says.

"Don't push me, b'y—I got no use for bullies. I see you on this stretch of road again, I'll call the cops and tell 'em what you did today. Assault. And I'll make darn sure it sticks."

"Yeah? You don't even know my name."

"I might look dumb as a hen, but I ain't. You're Hud Quinn from Fiddlers Cove and Fiddlers Cove's where you better stay. Git, now."

Hud kicks me hard on the shin. Then he picks up his bike and drives away.

I rub my face on my sleeve, get up on all fours, and scramble to my feet. Abe's field sways in front of my eyes, then settles. Abe is standing by the side of the road, an old shotgun under his arm.

"You okay, kid?"

"Would you really have shot Hud?" My voice sounds like I've got bronchitis.

Abe grins. He has gaps in his teeth. "None too easy when there's no shells in the gun."

Lucy's still barking from behind the fence. I lean over, needles of pain stabbing my chest, and drag my bike out of the ditch.

"Thanks," I mumble.

"You the doc's kid?" I nod. "You taken a shine to Gulley Cove?"

"Uh...yessir."

"Haunted, they say. By fishermen lost in a squall forty years back. You believe in ghosts?"

"Not in daylight, I don't."

He cackles. "See any cats down there?"

"A few."

"Good for nothing, them cats. Figured by now they'd be long dead."

He couldn't care less, that's plain as the dirt on his dungarees. The volcano's seething around inside me, even though Abe's the one who just rescued me and I ought to feel grateful.

"Who owned them?"

"No one that I calls to mind. They used to live off fish scraps from the boats." He spits on the ground. "No boats last five, six years. No fish. No scraps."

"The cats are starving—I've been taking them food."

"Feed 'em and you just get more. Let 'em starve, that's what I say."

"That's cruel!" Not that I jumped at the chance to feed them.

He shrugs. "They're cats. Not folk. How'll you get there in winter? Road drifts in bad."

"I don't know."

"That there bike'll be as much use as a sprung dory."

Snow's a big problem, for sure, but it's not the only one. When hockey begins, there'll be practices once or twice a week and tournaments on weekends.

My heart's sinking right down to my sneakers. I take another of those shallow breaths, trying to act cool, like I'm in total control of the situation.

But Abe's sneering at me—city kid who doesn't know up from down. I look him right in the eye. "Will you do me a favor?"

"Depends." The dog's barking again. "Shut up, Lucy!"

Lucy shuts up. "Will you give me a few of those old boards you got stashed against your shed? I noticed them the other day."

"What's it worth to ya?"

"I haven't got any money. I'm spending it all on cat food."

"You want a handout, you go to the Sally Ann," he says.

"I'll walk your dog."

"She'd pull you clear to Corner Brook and back."

"I'll shovel your path and front steps when it snows."

"How many boards d'you want?" Abe says.

"I can only carry six or seven."

"You take seven boards, you shovel seven times."

You old skinflint. No wonder you live out here all by yourself. "Okay," I say. I can get up early on school days and do it then.

"I'll come with you so's you take the right boards."

"I don't want rotten ones."

"Sassy, ain't ya?"

As Abe unlatches the gate, a growl rumbles in Lucy's throat. I eye her uneasily. She's a big dog, toffee-colored, her tail like Rayleen's feather duster. But when I step in, she backs off.

"She don't bother with pint-sized kids," Abe says. He leads the way across the grass to the shed, me close on his heels. Lucy trots behind, sniffing my ankles like she hasn't had breakfast.

"What d'you want the boards for?" he says.

"To fix the wharf where I fell in."

"Your dad know what you're up to?"

"No. You going to tell him?"

"Bad feel to that place," Abe says. "If you was smart, you'd forget about Gulley Cove and them cats."

"I can't," I say. It's a relief to tell the truth for once.

He slings several short boards in a pile. "Okay, buddy, these are yours. Got nails? Know which end of a hammer's which?"

"I'll figure it out."

"I'll loan you some rope to tie the wood to your bike. You bring it back, though."

"Great...thanks."

Abe mutters something under his breath and picks up the wood. Five minutes later the boards are fixed to the back of my bike with some classy knots he tied without even watching what he was doing.

"Will you teach me how to tie those?" I say, then wonder what the frig I'm getting into.

He straightens. "We'll see how good you shovel. Don't fall off the wharf."

Twice in a week? No way.

My knees have stiffened up from falling off the bike, and the wind catches at the boards, so it's hard pedaling. I park the bike near the first shack and untie the wood. Then I feed the cats, although Felix is the only one I see.

The boards are either too long or too short, I don't have a saw, and hitting a nail with a hammer isn't as easy as it looks. Twice in a row I bang my left thumb so hard it turns red and swells up. But eventually I get two boards nailed over the hole where I fell in. Then I look around for my gloves. They're gone.

I put them on the wharf. I know I did.

When I look over the edge of the wharf, the gloves are down below, soggy but still floating. A gust of wind must have blown them into the sea. The water's too deep for me to wade in and get them, even if I wasn't scared of the undertow.

I've done nothing but get in trouble since the day I saw the white cat streak across the wharf.

Hud's more than enough for a guy to deal with. He must have been lying in wait for me; that's twice he's caught me near Abe's. Add the days getting shorter, the temperature dropping, and two feet of snow, and you've got a major screw-up on your hands. I should've thought this whole thing through before I began feeding the cats.

Dad's got a point with Think Before You Act.

Don't I hate it when he's right.

But if I ask him for help, he'll have a fit that I've biked to Gulley Cove six different times, plus told all those lies. With Dad, you can't pretend a lie's just a fib—that's like calling double pneumonia a cold.

Sitting out of the wind, I eat part of my lunch to cheer myself up. Next, I hammer the rest of the boards over holes in the fourth shack. The final thing on the list is to check the roofs of the shacks.

The last three have too many loose shingles, so I take the hammer to the padlock on the first shack, because that looks like the tightest roof of all. The padlock's rusty but it doesn't give an inch, and the screws are in tight. I don't have a screwdriver and the hammer won't lever them out.

Right about now the kids will be heading for Pete's Halloween party. Pizza, horror movies, and cake. Feeling left out of things is a new one on me. On Willow Lane, there were always other kids around, friendly kids who liked me and invited me to their parties.

I blow my nose, sneak into the fourth shack, shake one of the food bowls, and sit down on the coil of rope. I'll do my meditating-monk-act and see what happens.

About ten minutes later, Felix puts his head through the gap. He sees me right away and hisses. I keep quiet. He marches in, his fur all puffed up, and stands there, howling and groaning like he's one of those drowned fishermen. "*Eeeeoooowww…*"

"Travis?" a voice quavers. "Is that you?"

I jump, the hair standing up on the back of my neck. Felix whips through the gap like a shell from Abe's gun.

The ghosts know my name.

Ten

Day 351...Mothers

"Travis, where'd you go?"

It's a girl's voice. Letting out my breath in a long *whoosh*, I creep over to the wall and peer between two boards. Prinny Murphy's standing on the wharf. Although she looks scared, she's showing no signs of taking off up the hill like Hud and Marty.

I crawl out and stand up. "What are you doing here?"

"I come to see what you're up to."

"How'd you know where to find me?"

"I been watching you," she says. "Last couple days."

"Spying on me! Why don't you get lost?"

"I can stand on this here wharf, too. What happened to your face? It's right dirty."

"Did you tell anyone I've been coming here?"

"Like who?" she says.

"Your parents."

"Right. Like I'm gonna tell my da what's going on in Gulley Cove."

"What about your mother?"

She shrinks into her windbreaker. It's thin, with frayed cuffs. Not warm like my fleece.

"Don't you gimme grief about my ma."

"I wasn't—"

"The whole of Ratchet knows about Ma and ain't backward in telling me," she says, her mouth sulky. "Anyways, where's *your* ma? Why didn't she come here along with you and your da?"

"She's dead."

Here I am, telling Prinny Murphy about Mum when I haven't told anyone else. While I was working on Mrs. Dooks's project, I acted like mothers had never been invented.

"Oh," Prinny says. "When did she die?"

"A year ago." Thirteen months, but who's counting.

"What happened?"

"She got sick." A big wave dashes itself against the rocks. "Only time I ever saw your mother was outside the store that day—does she drink a lot?"

Prinny kicks at a loose board. Her sneakers aren't Nikes or New Balance, they're the cheap kind from Wal-Mart. "On and off. More on than off these days. Booze. Moonshine. Whatever she can lay her hands on. She even tried mouthwash once, but it made her puke."

A lot of things click into place. Monday to Friday, Prinny's school lunches are two slices of white bread with peanut butter. Her ponytail's long and greasy. She's never invited to hang around with the other girls. So is it better to have a mum who's alive but doesn't look after you, or a mum who loved you and died?

"Back home, my Uncle George gets drunk four times a year," I say. "November Eleventh, Tib's Eve, Valentine's Day, and Canada Day. Rum on the rocks."

Prinny's mouth and shoulders droop. "Ma's a wild card...regular would be nice."

I have to take that look off her face. "There's a bunch of cats here at the cove," I say. "Wild ones. I've been feeding them."

"That's the noise I heard?" she says, perking up. "A cat?"

"His name's Felix. After the goalie."

I can tell she's never heard of Felix Potvin. "How many cats?" she says.

"Felix, Blackie, Ghost, Patches, Rocky, a little ginger one I've only seen twice, and another gray one I haven't got a name for, either."

"Maybe I could name them."

"Blackie's going to have kittens. You could take one."

For a moment her whole face shines. Then it shuts down like the plug's been pulled on the Christmas lights.

"Da wouldn't let me."

I don't much like the sound of either of her parents. "If we crawl into the shack and keep still, one of the cats might come in to eat."

"Let's," she says.

So we sit together on the coil of rope, her hugging her knees to keep warm. It feels okay to have someone else there, even though she's a girl and six inches taller than me. I'll say one thing; she knows how to stay still.

I'm about ready to give up when Blackie slinks through the gap. She sees us, stops, her nose twitching, then heads for the bowl, and buries her face in it. Prinny's grinning from ear to ear. This is the first time I've seen her smile; she looks almost pretty.

Blackie eats and eats, then she goes through her washing routine. Her coat's shinier now and not so matted. After a while, she gets up, stretches, and walks out as calm as if she owns the place.

"I wish I could have a kitten," Prinny says.

Seems like she's wishing for a kitten the same way I wish I was back in St. John's. Really hard, but you know it isn't going to happen.

"If I keep one, you can come and see it."

"Okay," she says, but I don't think she believes me.

As we go outside, we catch a glimpse of Rocky darting under a tree. "That's likely where they sleep," I say and walk toward the end shack to check on my gloves. They're caught between two rocks now, swaying back and forth like dead fish.

"Them yours?" Prinny says.

"They blew off the wharf."

"We can get 'em. There's a gaff in the shack."

"A gaff?"

"You spear fish with a gaff," she says. She disappears into the fourth shack and comes back out with a long pole that has a rusty hook and a point at one end. Leaning over, she snags the first glove and tosses it up on the wharf. Then she gets the second one.

"Wow," I say, "you've done that before."

"Da's a fisherman. He still goes out, lobster season."

I wring the water out of my gloves. "I'd have gotten in trouble over these...Thanks a lot, Prinny." Her cheeks go pink. "I didn't eat all my lunch," I add. "You want the rest?"

"P'raps."

I go over to my pack, which is leaning against the wall, and take out the lunch bag. When she sits down out of the wind and opens the bag, her eyes widen. "Ham and cheese. With real ham. You sure I can have it?"

"I'm not hungry." Lying again, but that's nothing new.

She chews slowly and thoroughly, like she's memorizing the taste. Then she eats the brownie, licking her fingers so she doesn't miss any of the icing.

"That was right good."

If peanut butter on white bread is her lunch, I don't want to know what supper is. "We should head back," I say. "I can't come tomorrow because Dad's home and I haven't told him I'm doing this. What about Monday after school?"

"I got chores," she says, "and remedial reading. Only time for me is weekends. Won't your dad whale the tar outta you if he finds out?"

"Nah…he'll talk on and on about trust and honesty until I want to crawl under the couch."

"It'll be a secret," she says, solemn like she's in church.

I wrap the wet gloves in the plastic bag and put them in my pack along with the hammer and nails, then we walk along the wharf together. At the bottom of the hill she says, "I cuts across the barrens to my place. See you, Travis."

"Bye, Prinny."

She trots off between the spruce trees and the rocks, her ponytail flapping. I already knew she was in remedial reading because Mrs. Dooks makes a point of mentioning it at least twice a week.

I get on my bike and ride home, keeping an eye out for Hud. There's a note on the door saying Rayleen's at her place and to come and get her. But first I put the hammer and nails away, throw the gloves in the dryer, and wash the dirt off my face. My muddy jeans and fleece go in the clothes hamper. Lucky they didn't tear when I fell off my bike.

Mum always said you should look for the good in everyone. Hard to know where you'd begin with Hud Quinn.

❧

That night, Dad drives me to St. Fabien, where I go out by myself dressed as a ghost in an old white sheet. People give out neat stuff, and sometimes I join groups of other kids because no one knows who I am. So it's kind of fun. Then on Sunday, Grady and me talk on the phone, comparing how much loot we got.

Monday and Tuesday go smooth as apples. Hud stays in Fiddlers Cove, Abe waves at me as I drive past, and Lucy wags her tail. Felix and Blackie both eat in the shack while I'm there, and I catch a glimpse of the little ginger cat and Rocky. One of Rocky's ears is torn, like he was in a fight. But he's not limping anymore.

Doesn't look like anyone went near the cove on Halloween.

At supper on Tuesday—roast chicken, another of my absolute favorites—Dad says, "I can get off early on Friday and meet you in St. Fabien after school. We could go to the snowmobile dealers to look around, then go back the next day when we've decided what we want."

I spear a couple of peas on my fork. If we do that on Friday and Saturday, I'll have to give the cats enough food on Thursday to last until Sunday. Maybe I could ask Prinny to feed them on Saturday.

Prinny's sort of like a stray cat herself.

"Hello," Dad says. "Anyone home?"

"That'd be great." No way I'll be able to sneak off to Gulley Cove on the new snowmobile.

"Are you okay, Travis?"

"Sure," I say and try to pay attention. "Will we be getting gear as well? Suits and gloves? Helmets?"

"You bet. They have hand warmers built into the handlebars, and tether cords so the snowmobile doesn't run away if you fall off." Dad grins. "We had an old Ski-Doo when I was a kid, but it was for hauling wood. This one's for fun."

If it wasn't for the cats, I'd be excited, too.

That night when I have a shower, I check the bruises on my knees. They're a mix of purple, pink, green, and yellow, like they're saying, *Cheer up, Hud's not that bad.*

Eleven

Day 346...7 Cats x 9 Lives

On Thursday, grades five and six visit the museum at the far end of St. Fabien. Mrs. Dooks told us about a polar bear that wandered into town, tried to get in someone's house, and got himself shot. Now he's stuffed, and they keep him in the museum. I've never seen a polar bear, alive or dead.

The bus pulls in at the museum. Across the street is a low brick building with a sign that says St. Fabien Veterinary Clinic.

Once we're inside the museum, everyone milling around and talking, I slip out the door. Mr. Murphy's bent over in the bus, doing something to one of the seats. I race across the street and dive into the clinic.

A woman in a white coat is sitting behind the desk. "Can I help you?" she says.

"Are you the vet?"

"She's on the phone right now, but I'll tell her you're here. What's your name?"

"Travis." I shift my feet, expecting Mrs. Dooks to come after me any minute.

"You can wait in here," she says and leads me into a room that smells of disinfectant. The posters on the wall show flea eggs stuck to the strands of a carpet and heartworms that look like globs of cooked spaghetti.

"Hello, Travis. I'm Dr. Larkin."

She's got freckles and orange hair that's a mess of curls. I say the first thing on my mind. "Do cats have kittens without any help?"

"Usually, yes. Is your cat going to have kittens?"

"It's a cat I know. She's sort of wild."

"Is she feral?"

"Feral?" I don't know that word.

"Sometimes stray cats turn wild," she says, "or else they've been born in the wild. Is that what you mean?" I nod my head. "Is it just one cat or are there more?"

"More." I wish she'd stop asking so many questions.

She reaches for a pad and pen. "Where are they?"

"One of them's got a sore eye, all stuck together with yellow guck. Can you give me something to put on it? But I've only got $10.57."

"Travis, if it's a feral cat, you'll never get near enough to put anything on its eye. You'd better tell me where the cats are, and I'll come and take a look."

If she does that, Dad'll find out where I've been going after school. "Then what would you do?"

"Try and trap the cats. Bring them here, test for feline leukemia and, providing they don't have it, give them their shots."

"What if they do have it?"

She hesitates. "You can isolate a house cat for three months and retest it. But if it's a feral cat that's not in good shape, then we'd probably have to put it to sleep. Feline leukemia is a terrible disease and the cat gets very ill. Also, an infected cat can spread the disease to all the other cats—the same way that if you get a cold, you can give it to your friends."

Maybe Felix has feline leukemia. Or Blackie. They're not in great shape. So if the vet goes to Gulley Cove, the cats get killed. That's what she means.

"I'm supposed to be at the museum," I say. "I better go."

"Are you feeding the cats?"

I edge toward the door. "Yeah."

"I'd do my very best to look after them, because I hate to see animals suffering. Won't you tell me where they are—or at least give me your phone number?"

With my luck, Dad would answer. "I *can't*."

She's looking right at me, not mean like Mrs. Dooks, just determined. Then she flips through a pile of pamphlets on the counter and takes one out. "This is some information about feral cats. And here's my card. You can call me anytime."

The name on the card is Dr. Kelsey Larkin. "Thanks," I say, stuffing the information in my pocket as I rush out of the room. It's started to rain.

Mrs. Dooks is standing at the front door of the museum, tapping her foot on the floor. "Where have you been, Travis? I've been searching everywhere for you."

"Sorry, Mrs. Dooks."

"If you needed to talk to the vet, you should have asked."

Like she'd have let me. "Yes, Mrs. Dooks."

"You'll stay indoors at lunchtime tomorrow and write a one-page essay on reliability."

Feeding the cats is all about reliability. I slouch off to join the other kids. The polar bear's a bummer because it's losing its fur and its eyes are made of black glass.

I read the pamphlet on the bus that afternoon. To prevent kittens being born in the wild, it says, the cats are neutered. Then they're often put back where they came from because they're so difficult to tame.

I can't see what good that does.

The rest of the way home I stare at the raindrops smearing the window.

By the time I reach Gulley Cove on my bike, my jacket's wet through. The cats' bowls are full of water from leaks in the roof. The roof on the first shed is in great shape, but the door's shut tight. Because Rayleen hassled me about going for a ride in the rain, I forgot to bring a screwdriver, so I try and break the padlock with a rock.

Doesn't make a dent in it.

If I had a saw and knew how to use it, I could make a cat door in the wall so Blackie could go in and out. For Abe to lend me a saw, I'd probably have to shovel his roof.

Useless. That's me. City kid who can score goals but can't bust open the door on an old fish shack.

The cats are like a big weight that I'm lugging around and can't put down. They need shelter for the winter. Felix's eye is still gucky. If anything goes wrong with Blackie and her kittens, I don't know what to do. I don't even know how I'm going to get down here when it snows. But now if I tell Dad about the cats, Dr. Larkin'll come out, and maybe Felix and Blackie and the rest of them'll have that disease. Feline leukemia.

Seven cats. Each one losing all nine lives at once.

Twelve

Day 345...Not an Option

On Friday after school, Dad's waiting for me in the Toyota. It feels like a vacation. No biking to Gulley Cove, no worrying about Hud or the cats. Prinny said she'd feed them on Saturday. She liked being asked. When I warned her about Hud, she said she can run faster than him.

We drive down the street to the first snowmobile dealer and I forget all about Gulley Cove. I want every Ski-Doo in the place. Yellow ones, blue ones, ones that'll climb mountains or pull sleds with a winter's load of wood. Racing brakes, 1000cc engines, 16″ tracks—everything shiny and new. Dad's trying to act like a grown-up but he's worse than me.

My head's spinning by the time we leave and walk down the street to the Pizza Hut. As we go past a hobby shop, Dad stops. "Isn't that the remote control car you wanted?"

On a shelf in the window is a black SUV with hand controls. I look at it longingly.

"Yeah."

"Why don't you buy it?"

Spent my money on cat food, Dad. "Maybe I'll wait a while."

"It would keep you out of mischief after school."

My heart thuds like I just bumped into Hud in a dark alley. Does Dad know about Gulley Cove? I sneak a glance at him, but he's busy reading the labels on the box. "I like riding my bike when I get off the bus," I say. "I bet they've never opened a window in that school since it was built."

"How much allowance have you saved up?"

"Let's go, Dad. I'm hungry and we want to go to the Arctic Cat dealer after supper."

He's looking at me kind of funny. Not downright suspicious but heading that way. He doesn't say anything, though, until we're in the restaurant and they've brought our drinks. Coke for me and coffee for him.

"You remember when we decided to come here that only one house was for rent, the one we're living in now?" he says. "I found out today that a patient of mine is moving away for a few months. We could rent her house here in St. Fabien. You wouldn't have to take the school bus anymore, and you'd be near the rink when hockey starts."

I poke my straw in the Coke and watch the bubbles burst. If we moved to St. Fabien, I wouldn't have to put up with Hud on the bus twice a day. But the cats would starve. I've been feeding them for over a week now, so they're used to it. *Putting meat on their bones*, Rayleen would say. "I don't want to move again."

"I'm not sure Ratchet is the best place for you. Hardly any kids there…Rayleen says you don't bring anyone home after school, just take off on your bike by yourself. You'd find it easier to make friends in St. Fabien."

"I'm making friends in Ratchet," I say, wondering what Prinny would think if she could hear me.

"Think about it over the weekend."

"I don't need to."

The waitress brings our pizza, thin-crust Hawaiian. "So the experiment's working for you?" Dad says.

It's the first time he's asked.

I take a big wedge loaded with pineapple and ham. Hud scares the bejasus out of me, Mrs. Dooks hates kids, cranky old Abe's got me shoveling his path, and a girl whose mother's the town drunk knows I'm stuck with seven half-starved cats.

"Yeah," I say, "it's working."

"We'll have fun on the snowmobile this winter."

"If we had snowshoes, I could go out on the barrens on my own. Not out of sight of the houses; you've got rules about that. But I might see caribou again."

Dad chews thoughtfully. "So you really like it in Ratchet." He has that look on his face that says *I know something's going on, but I haven't quite figured out what it is yet.*

"Snowshoes would be fun," I say.

"Christmas is coming."

I'll need them before Christmas, although I can't tell him that. "Can I go to the salad bar?"

"Sure," Dad says. "I'll join you in a minute."

It's on the other side of the room. As I reach for a plate, I see Hector Baldwin standing there, his plate piled high with macaroni, iceberg lettuce, and those little ears of corn.

"Hi," I say. "You here with your mum and dad?"

"Yep," Hector says.

I grab the edge of the counter like I'm about to faint. "Hey, you used a real word...so you *can* talk. You been shopping?"

"Deal's Hardware."

"Why don't you ever talk to me on the bus?"

"Hud," he says.

For a moment our eyes meet and Hud Quinn links us together as if we're the best of friends. Then Hector shifts his feet.

"Gotta go."

I load my plate with potato salad and pickled beets and go back to our table.

Dad and I check out the Arctic Cat dealer, then we go home.

Thirteen

Day 344...Fathers

While Dad's having his morning shower, I ride over to Prinny's place with a box of cat food in a plastic bag. Her father opens the door. He's tall, like Dad, with enough flesh on him to bait a whole school of trout. Even though it's Saturday and the sun's shining, he doesn't look any too happy. His overalls are greasy and his hair needs washing, like Prinny's.

Maybe hair only gets washed when other stuff's okay, I think, remembering Blackie's fur. "Is Prinny home?"

"Who are you?"

"Travis Keating. From down the road."

"The doc's kid." Prinny's dad can do suspicious big time, way better than my dad. "What do you want Prinny for?"

I take a step backward; by the looks of him, Prinny could get in trouble for breathing. "Something I want to ask her."

He bellows, "Prinny!"

She comes on the run from the kitchen. "Hi, Travis. It's okay, Da, we goes on the bus together. I'll finish up the dishes later."

He lumbers off. She edges out on the step. "Hide the cat food behind the shed. I'll feed them this afternoon once my chores are done." Then she smiles like she knows it's a sunny Saturday, and I forget that her ponytail needs shampooing and smile back.

"I don't want you getting in trouble," I say.

"If he asks, I'll tell him you brought some homework."

More lies. Those cats have a lot to answer for.

"I can go to Gulley Cove tomorrow. Can you?"

"There's Mass at ten, then I cooks dinner. I'll come to your place around one-thirty."

I tuck the cat food in some dead grass behind the shed and bike home. Seems like I told Dad the truth for once, and I really am making a friend in Ratchet.

A girl.

She doesn't care that I'm a city kid.

That afternoon, Dad and me drive to St. Fabien again, and he buys a Ski-Doo, a black two-seater with a four-stroke engine. We get a trailer and all the gear, and drive home pulling it behind us. Awesome.

Dad backs the trailer into the driveway and un-hitches it. We walk around the Ski-Doo a few times, admiring the shocks, the luggage compartment, the foot rests, you name it. I catch Dad stroking the wind-shield. He looks embarrassed, then he starts to laugh. We both end up leaning against the trailer laughing like fools.

Haven't done that in a long time.

Wiping his eyes, Dad says, "Now all we need is a foot of snow."

This brings me down with a thud. Dad didn't buy snowshoes.

Stealing five quarters is one thing. Stealing a Ski-Doo is a whole different ballgame.

Fourteen

Day 343...Lava

Sunday morning's mild enough for me to wash the Toyota. Dad pays me ten bucks, which means I'm set for cat food for a while.

When I call Grady after lunch, his mother answers. She's nice. She used to talk to me about Mum sometimes, saying things like, "Remember how Susan loved my bakeapple preserves?" Or, "Susan's favorite color was sunshine yellow." Although it made me sad, it was an okay kind of sad because we were remembering Mum. Here, no one talks about her, so she feels a long way away.

I often wish I'd kept the Big Yell to myself.

Grady's out playing ball hockey with the other boys, his mother says. She'll get him to call me when he comes in. I put the phone down, feeling the same as when I wasn't invited to Pete's Halloween party. Grady's got lots of friends.

I've got seven cats and a girl with dirty hair. *Her* mother's not nice.

At quarter past one, someone knocks on the front door. I'm in the back porch searching for a screwdriver, so by the time I get to the door, Dad's opening it. Prinny looks up at him like he's God and she's been struck dumb.

"Dad, this is Prinny Murphy," I say. "We're going out. We'll be back before dark."

"I gotta have supper on the table for five," she whispers.

"Nice to meet you, Prinny," Dad says, smiling at her. She blushes. Then he says, "Stay in sight of the houses, Travis. Have you got your watch?"

"Yeah. We'll be back by four. Let's go, Prinny."

We head out behind the house so Prinny can show me her shortcut to Gulley Cove. It angles across the barrens, then sinks down into the trees behind the cove. We go single file, so we don't talk much. She picks her way through the rocks, nimble as a caribou and almost as fast. I stumble along behind her. No matter how hard I try to put my sneakers where she just put hers, I can't seem to manage it.

The other day I hinted around the subject of Prinny's mother to Rayleen. Rayleen raised her eyebrows clear to the ceiling. "That woman? Soused like a mackerel even on Sundays. She's a Quinn from Fiddlers Cove. No good ever come of that crew."

I've seen Hud Quinn's place when the school bus stops in Fiddlers Cove to pick him up. A beat-up house with cross-eyed windows. A shed out back, tarpaper peeling off the walls. Two wrecked cars in the yard, along with an old wringer washer and a mud-colored couch with springs sticking out like corkscrews.

If Prinny's mother is a Quinn, I bet Prinny's related to Hud. So why would I want *her* for a friend?

Trouble is I'm desperate for someone to treat me half-decent. Anyone, anytime—starting with recess. Recess feels like I'm stranded on the ice in Antarctica with no one sending out an expedition to look for me.

Total misfit, that's me.

Unlike Dad. He's not stifled anymore. He whistles when he showers, like he used to before Mum got sick, and he's smiling when he drives off to the clinic.

"Watch the hole."

"Huh?"

"You gotta keep your mind on the path," Prinny says.

"Don't tell me what to do!"

"Someone's got to—you're clumsy as a sick cow."

"Didn't anyone ever teach you any manners?"

Her voice rises like the high tide. "So I'm good

80

enough to feed the cats so long as you don't have to pass the time of day with me?"

"I never said that." Although I was thinking it. I kick the nearest boulder. I could kick it fifty times and it wouldn't notice. My toe's what would hurt.

"It's 'cause I'm a girl, right? Or is it 'cause my ma's a drunk?"

"I don't care about your ma."

"Yeah, right."

"You're not Grady! That's what's wrong."

She wipes her nose on her sleeve, scowling at me. "Who's Grady?"

"My best friend. He lives on our street in St. John's, at 18 Willow Lane." I kick the boulder again, harder this time so my toe does hurt.

"I never had a best friend. You don't know how lucky you are."

"What's the good when he's miles away?"

"I bet he misses you."

"He's out playing ball hockey with Dave and Alex. He doesn't miss me."

"Oh," Prinny says. "That's too bad."

"I don't need you feeling sorry for me."

She brings the end of her ponytail around and starts chewing on it. "You're too busy feeling sorry for yourself."

"I am *not*."

"What you need is a good swift kick in the arse."

Arse was right up there with *ain't* as far as Mum was concerned, and suddenly the volcano inside me erupts.

"I hate it here! I hate going on the school bus. I hate Hud Quinn and Marty Dunston and grouchy old Mrs. Dooks. I hate having no place to go and no friends and no mother and I hate your dirty hair—I wish you'd go home and wash it!"

Prinny looks like I just slapped her in the face. But she doesn't cry. Without saying a word, she turns on her heel and heads up the path, walking at first, then trotting, then running, dodging among the rocks as if a pack of wolves was after her. A few minutes later, she vanishes over the top of the hill.

A chickadee calls from the spruce trees and another one answers. Chickadees always sound upbeat to me, like nothing can go wrong with the world.

Boy, are they screwed up.

I'm the one who screwed up.

I sit down on the nearest boulder and stare at the ocean. The water rushes in, smashes on the rocks, and rushes out again.

I remember how Prinny fished each glove out of the sea with a flick of her wrist, and how she smiled when I thanked her. Then I remember how back home Jasper Hines threw Samantha Weir's pink Barbie book bag in a mud puddle last spring and tromped on it, and how Samantha didn't cry but just stared at him like the end of the world had come.

Doesn't matter that Prinny's bigger than me. I pulled a Jasper on her. Or, worse, a Hud.

Bully for you, Travis. Ha, ha.

After a while I feed the cats. Then I walk home along the road, even though it's longer than across the barrens, because I don't want to meet up with Prinny. She'll be on the bus tomorrow. That's soon enough.

But the next day when the bus pulls up by her place, her father hollers from the front step, "She's sick."

Mr. Murphy waves, bangs the door shut and we drive to Hector's. Maybe she's sick because I was mean to her. Or her dad found out she went to Gulley Cove and punished her. Whaled the tar outta her.

I scrunch down in my seat. It's me who feels sick.

That afternoon, when I'm climbing on the bus, Hud kicks the feet out from under me and I bang my elbow on the step. Only bright spot in the whole day is that the parts have arrived for the Zamboni and hockey'll start this week.

I fed the cats plenty the day before, so I take the day off, playing *Star Wars II* in my room while Rayleen watches the soaps. She doesn't believe in kids' rights. When she wants the TV, she gets it.

I blast a couple of droids so they explode in smoke, then zap another one, pretending he's Hud. The experiment's just for a year, and then we'll go back to St. John's. Why should I care what a girl with dirty hair thinks about me?

Fifteen

Day 341...White, Gray, Black

Prinny gets on the bus the next morning. She keeps her hood up because it's cold, and she doesn't look my way, not once. If I apologized to her, she'd look at me. I should just do it.

Maybe I've gotten so used to being on my own that I can't be bothered.

I stare out the window, where the sky and the sea are a matching dull gray. At recess it starts to snow. The kids are talking about a blizzard, even though the snowflakes are drifting down like they're in no hurry to go anywhere.

School gets out an hour early because by now the snow's settling fast, the flakes so thick you can hardly see the road. Mr. Murphy drives slow, the wipers swishing back and forth as he peers through the windshield.

I wish I'd fed the cats yesterday. I have to go today, snow or no snow.

Rayleen's not at the house yet. I leave her a note telling her I've gone sledding, and pull on my new snowmobile suit and the gloves Prinny fished out of the sea. In the shed there's a wooden toboggan, which whizzes me down the hills, although slugging uphill isn't much fun. It's exciting to be out in the storm, though, the wind driving spray on the rocks like Star Wars explosions.

At Gulley Cove, there's not a cat in sight.

Snow's already piling into the last two shacks. I lug a couple of small barrels out of the end shack and roll them into the fourth one, fighting the wind, testing the wharf with each step. After up-ending the barrels near the two biggest gaps in the walls, I cover them with an old canvas that's crusted with fish scales. Then I wedge plywood between the second barrel and the wall to make a shelter in one corner, and pour out enough food for an army of cats.

Next time the kids at school say *blizzard*, I'll pay more attention.

Outside the shed, the wind thrusts me sideways as though I don't weigh any more than Ghost. The snow's falling thicker now, muffling the roar of the surf. "There's lots of food in here!" I shout, but the gale grabs my voice and throws it out to sea, where the waves are flinging themselves around as if they're having a fit.

The first shack wavers in and out of sight. By the time I reach it, I'm out of breath and I'm afraid.

Deep down afraid.

It's getting dark. No point standing here holding onto the wall like it's the only solid thing between me and Abe's.

I leave the toboggan where it is because it's almost buried, and step out into the wind. Frozen spray stings my cheek. Bringing one glove up for protection, ducking my head, I set off. The first hill isn't too bad because the wind's from behind, butting me along like the kids in the locker room at lunch hour. The wind's a big bully. Like Hud. When he's tormenting someone, he looks as near to happy as he's likely to get.

If only I hadn't told Prinny to go home and wash her hair.

At the crest of the hill, the gale slams into me. The storm's not exciting anymore; it's out of control. Which is when I learn—not for the first time—that if you push *exciting* too far, it flips into *dangerous*.

Head down, I plow through the drifts. All these snowflakes and each one's different—that's what we learned in science class. I bet more snowflakes are flying around the track than there are people in the world, including Manhattan and Mexico City.

Including Prinny and Hud and me.

The hollow at the bottom of the hill has drifted in, nearly to my waist. For a moment I gape at it, paralyzed, snow sifting between my lips and melting on my tongue. Shuffling my feet with each step, thrusting snow out of the way with my hands, I start across. Getting to the other side is like hiking two kilometers in goalie gear.

The wind has scraped bare patches on the uphill slope, flakes whipping around so fast they look like ghosts, the kind that are out to get you. The level part of the road's a killer because I can't always see the tuckamore—the only thing between me and the cliffs.

I swing my arms, picture Rayleen putting brownies in the oven, and keep going. One foot after the other. Boots vanishing in the snow. Knees aching, a stitch in my side.

Every now and then, through a gap in the snow, I can see waves breaking on the shore in big bursts, white in a black sea with no colors in between. I used to think telling lies was like that; lies are bad, truth's good. Dead easy.

Won't be so easy to lie my way out of this one.

What's that gray patch right in front of me?

I leap back, stumble, and fall sideways onto solid

ground. I'm hugging it, terror like a sickness in my throat.

The gray patch was empty air.

I nearly fell off the cliff.

No one would have found me for days. If ever.

Snow's melting on my cheek and running down inside my collar. A sob pushes its way out, then another. I'm falling apart, like the day the undertow got me.

Funeral Face. Slap it on fast.

I struggle to my knees. Only one more hill left, the one that leads up to Abe's place. I crawl farther away from the cliff, stagger upright, and start walking, testing the ground with each step. One foot, then the other, over and over again.

I'm partway up the hill when a light appears at the top, dim through the snow, flickering in and out. It moves closer, getting brighter all the time. I gape at it, wondering if I'm hallucinating.

It's a snowmobile. A black one like ours, going slow down the hill, the engine roaring louder than the wind.

It *is* ours. Dad's driving, standing up to see where he's going. Oh man, am I in for it. The clinic must have closed early, and that's how he found out I was gone.

The headlight picks me out, blinding me. Dad turns off the ignition, leaps off the Ski-Doo, and wades the last few feet through the drifts. Putting his arms around me, he lifts me off my feet and hugs me so hard that what breath I've got left is squeezed out of me.

"Travis, are you okay?"

I can't seem to find my voice, so I nod against his chest. He pushes me away so he can look at my face. "Where in *hell* have you been? I was worried sick when I got home and you weren't there." Then he hugs me again.

When Dad swears, watch out. It doesn't happen often, but it means business.

Not waiting for an answer, he plunks me down on the back seat of the snowmobile, sits down himself, and yells, "Hold on!" I grab him around the waist. Sitting feels weird, like I might never stand up again.

The snowmobile growls into action, churning up the hill and past Abe's place. Dad keeps to the edge of the road, then turns into our driveway. After he parks by the side of the house, he hits the kill switch.

I don't think I can move.

I slide to the ground, get my balance, and head for the front door. Dad unlocks it. Every leg muscle I own seizes up as I go inside.

The light's too bright, and it's awful quiet now we're out of the wind. "I was watching some caribou," I say. "They were close because they were upwind and didn't know I was there. Then I saw three ptarmigan digging in the snow and forgot about the time. Sorry, Dad."

"Sorry doesn't cut it. I'll give Rayleen a call to let her know you're safe, then we'll eat. Hang up your gear."

The snow's melting from my eyebrows and trickling down my face. I shake my suit, hang it on a hook, and bang my boots on the mat.

Now there'll be fifteen rules about blizzards.

I'm never going to tell anyone about the cliff.

Rayleen left pork chops and gravy in the pan, along with mashed potatoes and broccoli. Broccoli's my least favorite vegetable. I give us one chop each, put two scoops of potato on each plate, and divide up the broccoli.

Dad gets off the phone. We sit down. He says, his eyes pinning me to the chair, "We'll eat first and talk later," and attacks his pork chop like it's me he's cutting into little pieces.

I eat the broccoli first.

Dessert's blueberry pie. Kind of a waste because I'm too revved up to taste it.

"Put the dishes in the sink," Dad says. "You can wash them later."

Cutlery into a mug of hot water. Bones in the garbage. Rinse the plates clean, watching how the blueberry juice turns the water purple as a bruise. Poke bits of food out of the sink plug and drop them in the garbage. Then there's nothing left to do but sit down again across from Dad. The clock's ticking over the sink and snow's hissing against the windows.

"You're grounded," Dad says.

Grounded. No one to feed the cats.

"I can see you don't like the idea." He leans forward. "You scared me out of ten years' growth. You could have got lost on the barrens and frozen to death."

"How long am I grounded?"

"A week."

Not as long as I expected. But I'm already afraid that snow will have gotten through the holes in the roof and covered up the food dishes; I can't stay away for seven whole days. "Hockey starts this week," I say.

"You won't be going. No TV and no videos. No treats at the store. If I can't rely on you to be sensible, you won't be allowed on the barrens at all—for God's sake, Travis, I was ready to call the police and have them send out a search party."

A blueberry skin's stuck between my teeth; I worry at it with my tongue. If it wasn't for the stupid vet, I might tell Dad the truth. He's supposed to heal stuff, so wouldn't he think it was a good idea to be feeding the cats? But I can't stand the thought of them being put to sleep if they've got that disease.

Dad sighs. "I'm glad you're taking an interest in the wildlife on the barrens," he says, "and that you're settling down here. But you've got to smarten up—I have

92

to go to work and I can't be fretting over you every minute of the day."

He's waiting for me to say something. "Okay, Dad." Then I think of something else. "I promised Abe Murphy I'd shovel for him. How am I going to do that if I'm grounded?"

"It's because you told me you hurt your hand near Abe's that I went looking for you up there. You should have thought about the shoveling before you stayed out so late."

"It was a promise, Dad."

Dad's as big on keeping promises as he is on keeping the rules. He gives another of those who-wants-to-be-a-father sighs. "You can get up early and do it before you catch the bus."

"Thanks," I say and escape to wash the dishes.

By bedtime, the blizzard still hasn't let up.

Sixteen

Day 340...Escape Artist

In the morning, the sky's bright blue, as if it had never heard of snow. The plow's been through in the night, so it doesn't take me long to get to Abe's. The whole way there I'm in a stew about Gulley Cove; I keep seeing Felix's ugly mug and Blackie's swollen belly. I have to feed them, they're depending on me. But how am I going to get there?

Lucy has peed in the drifts, little holes with yellow rims. When I push on the gate, Abe opens the front door.

"Up early, b'y. Some mess o' snow, eh?"

Lucy lunges toward me, like she's the snowplow. I've always wanted a big dog without stopping to think that big means *big*. Teeth included. I hold out my hand. "Good girl." She wags her tail, sniffing my boots as though she knows I've been feeding cats. "Abe," I say, "have you got any snowshoes?"

"Used to. Gave them to me nephew last winter when he moved to Goose Bay."

So that's that. He passes out a shovel and I get to work. I do the best job I can, leave the shovel by the door, and rush home to catch the bus.

Prinny's the second one on, a wool hat pulled down over her ears. She gives me a quick look. It's no big deal to say *I'm sorry*, especially when I am, but Mr. Murphy's right there so I clam up. She turns away and gazes out the window.

Guilt's like the undertow at Gulley Cove—once it's got you, it works you over. *I hate your dirty hair...* now I see why people buy those time travel books where the hero goes back into the past and changes the way things happened.

Wish I could go backward and get rid of the snow. No point in wishing I had the nerve to take off on Dad's Ski-Doo. There's limits.

When I arrive home that afternoon, Rayleen looks up from the TV long enough to say, "That girl, Prinny Murphy, she left something for you yesterday. In the front porch."

At first I can't see anything in the porch. But tucked behind Dad's raincoat is a pair of homemade snowshoes with wooden tails and rubber bindings. I take them out and run my fingers over the knotted moose hide. I've never been so glad to see anything in my life.

Even though Prinny's mad at me, she's put the cats first. This morning she was probably wondering why I didn't thank her.

More guilt. Jeez.

Still wearing my jacket, I carry the snowshoes through the living room. Rayleen says, kind of snarky, "Snow'll be melted by the time you can use those."

Rayleen wouldn't feed the cats; she'd side with Abe.

"I'm going to listen to some music," I say and go to my room, closing the door. Last night I hid my old boots under the bed while Dad was in the bathroom. Now I stash three CDs in my player, turn Green Day on loud, and push the window up. I throw the snowshoes out and follow them into the snowdrift. Putting them on is tricky, and the first few steps I nearly fall flat on my face because they're longer than I expected. By taking bigger steps, I start to get the hang of them, and set off behind the house so Rayleen can't see me.

I follow Prinny's shortcut until the boulders start poking above the snow; then I angle over to the road, staying well away from the edge of the cliff. At Gulley Cove, a pattern of paw prints goes from the rocks to the fourth shack.

The barrels kept most of the snow out. There's a rusty spade leaning in one corner, so I use it to clear a path from the trees to the shack, talking to the cats the whole time. Before I leave, I catch a glimpse of Blackie and Felix among the rocks. "I left tons of food, guys, and I'll do my best to come back on the weekend. If I don't get caught today."

If Rayleen bangs on my door to offer me a brownie, or Dad phones home to check up on me, I'm history; I'll be grounded until I'm eighteen.

I cut across the barrens again, following the snow-shoe tracks, which look like two rows of fish lying head to tail. At the back of the house, Green Day's still blasting out the window. After I tug off the snowshoes and rap the snow from them, I clamber inside. Then I start easing the window down. It sticks part way, so I give it a sharp tap.

"Where've you been?"

The window frame bangs down, missing my fingers by half an inch.

"Think you're pretty smart, eh?"

It's not Rayleen or Dad—that much I know. I turn around. A young guy's propped against the doorframe. He's got studs in both ears, one nostril, and his lower lip. "I'm Matt," he says. "My kid brother cut his hand, so Ma had to drive him to the clinic—I'm filling in for her."

"Ma? You mean Rayleen?"

"Yep. Ain't you grounded?"

"Yeah."

He grins. One of his front teeth is chipped. The stud in his lip bobbing up and down, he says, "I been out a few windows in my day."

"You going to tell her?"

"You kidding?"

Am I in luck. "Will your brother be okay?"

"Sure—got careless with his army knife. Ma left cake out. Want some?"

So we end up stuffing ourselves with chocolate cake and ice cream and watching *The Simpsons.* When Dad gets home, Matt leaves, winking at me as he goes out the door. It's dark by now, which means Dad won't see the snowshoe tracks.

After supper, I rush through the dishes and my homework, and go to my room. After leafing through a magazine, I cut out a couple of pictures of cats, paste them on pink construction paper, and fold the paper to make a card. Then I pick up my pen.

I chew on it for four or five minutes. This is worse than social studies, when Mrs. Dooks says to write about "The Function of the Legislative Assembly."

I'm sorry I was mean to you, Prinny, I write. *Thanks a lot for lending me the snowshoes. Sincerely, Travis.*

No mention of Gulley Cove in case her dad reads it.

The card looks sort of bare with just the two cats. Adding a BMW, a bunch of tulips, and a dopey-looking grizzly bear who reminds me of Felix livens it up some.

I don't have an envelope big enough, so I wrap the card in a plastic Co-Op bag and tape the bag shut. Then I go into the living room, where Dad's watching football. "Prinny was sick and I made her a card," I say. Which is circling the truth. "Can I take it over there? I'll come right back."

"That girl looks like she could do with a good square meal," Dad says. "Fifteen minutes max."

I run to her place and bang on the door. Her dad opens it. He's got little burn holes in his T-shirt. "Is Prinny home?"

"Yeah. C'mon in." He shouts her name over the noise of wrestling on TV. The crowd's screaming as a fat guy in lime green tights pounds on another guy's arm. I've seen the fat guy before. His name's the Crusher.

Smells like Prinny and her dad had canned beans and wieners for dinner.

I'm worried she'll think the card is dumb. Or cowardly. Or both.

Prinny marches out of the kitchen. She looks taller than usual and I suddenly realize what's different. She's washed her hair—her ponytail's all shiny, curling at the ends. My face goes as red as the bleeding heart of Jesus in the picture on the wall.

I thrust the bag at her. "Can't stay. I'm grounded," I say, and hurry outside.

I'm home in nine minutes.

It snows in the night, hiding the snowshoe tracks.

Seventeen

Days 339 to 333...Out of the Cage

When Prinny gets on the bus the next morning, she's not wearing a hat. Her hair's still shiny. She sits across from me at the front like she always does.

"I liked the card a lot," she says, not looking at me. Then she takes out a grade four reader and buries her nose in it.

So the card *was* okay. More than okay—a stroke of genius.

We stop at Hector's and for the next few minutes, the bus is quiet and peaceful. In Fiddlers Cove, Hud gets on.

"Hi there," Mr. Murphy says.

Hud grunts like Hector. On his way past, he flicks out his palm and cracks me on the ear. My good mood shatters like the glass I dropped on the kitchen floor last week. I stare out the window and remember how

Grady and me used to walk the six blocks to school, kicking a soccer ball or passing a puck back and forth with our old hockey sticks.

Seems like a long time ago.

❧

Friday it warms up, the snow scrunching down as it melts. Sloppy brown mud edges the schoolyard, giving Mrs. Dooks something new to complain about. At recess, I search out Prinny. She's standing by the swings, watching the other girls giggle and gossip. I guess washing her hair didn't help any.

"Can you feed the cats on the weekend?" I say. "Twice, maybe? I'm grounded until next Wednesday."

"Sure," she says with a big smile. "I'll get off the bus at your place today and pick up the food."

"Thanks. Otherwise, they'd go hungry. But watch out for Hud—he sometimes hangs around Abe's."

"I'll go the shortcut—Hud don't like to walk."

So that's a big load off my mind.

Still, being grounded's no fun. You can only play *NHL* and *Need For Speed* so many times. I even haul out my old Lego set and build Batwing and the Joker Copter; I haven't done that for months. On Friday afternoon, Saturday morning, and Monday night, I try not to think about hockey practice, which is my only hope of connecting with Cole, Buck, and Stevie; I'll be in Peewee, like them.

Hud's in Bantam, so he can't touch me when I'm on the ice.

❧

Tuesday evening feels a million hours long. Then it's Wednesday and I'm free. The sun's shining, last night's snow is wet and slushy, and it feels like a big adventure to take the shortcut to Gulley Cove.

Melted snow's leaked through the roof of the fourth shack and dripped into the bowls, making cat food soup. I move the bowls to the dry patches on the floor and fill them. Then I sit down on the coil of rope and wait. Blackie walks in, gives me a look that says, *It took you long enough*, and starts to eat. I tell her about being grounded, and about Rayleen's son, Matt. "Rayleen's more interested in the soaps—in Mira, Flint, and Destiny—than in me. No use pretending she's anything like my mum."

Flitting her whiskers, Blackie picks up another piece of cat food. "Funny how I'm thinking more about Mum since we moved to Ratchet…At the wake, Uncle George got into the rum, said how she was down to skin and bones by the end. 'Like one of them fashion models,' which is when Dad told him to shut up. They were squaring off like a couple of prize-fighters, so the funeral director pushed another glass of rum at Uncle George and hustled Dad off to talk to Great-Aunt Gladys, who'd come all the way from Burgeo...I sometimes wonder if Uncle George is the reason Dad and Mum only had one kid."

Blackie sits back, yawns, and stretches. I move a little closer. She tenses, watching me, so I stay put until she swipes her paw over her face. Shifting a little at a time, sitting tight in between, I get within three feet of her. Then she pads outside, her belly swaying. It's bigger now. I don't know how many kittens she'll have, where she'll have them, or how I'll find homes for them. And how will I fix the roof when any time I pick up a hammer, it's my thumb that gets hit?

Ghost pokes his head in, sees me, and backs out fast. I sit down on the rope again and think, *Monk.* Felix is next. He growls at me, the fur on his neck standing up like a ruff.

I roll my eyes. "Come off it. You're not scared of the shortest kid in grade six."

As he settles in to eat, I try getting closer to him.

"*Eeeooouuwww...*" Worse than the wind in a blizzard. He doesn't run away, though. His eye isn't as gunky, but there's a new scratch on his nose. "Don't you dare have feline leukemia," I say. "You or any of the others—you hear me?" He eats some more, gives his tail a couple of passes with his tongue, then stalks out in his own good time.

I snowshoe home along the edges of the track, hauling the toboggan I left behind in the blizzard. The trees are hung with little drops like earrings. The ditches gurgle under the snow and the sea sighs like it feels lazy.

Abe's oiling the hinges on the gate. "Found some snowshoes, eh? Where you been the last few days?"

"Dad grounded me because I was out late the night of the storm."

"In my day you'd get whupped."

"Did you get whupped, Abe?"

"Didn't do me no harm."

I wasn't so sure. "Was the shoveling okay?"

"Six more storms and we're even."

"You gonna teach me to tie those knots?" I ask.

"You buttering me up so's you won't have to shovel again?"

"No! Do you always look for the worst in people?"

Abe scowls. "Your tongue flaps like long johns on a clothesline."

I scowl right back. "Gotta go home and go through my hockey gear. First practice on Friday."

"That mean you'll quit feeding them cats?"

"No more than you'll quit feeding Lucy."

He mutters something that sounds like *smartass*. Feeling like I just scored a hat trick, I say, "See you."

Eighteen

Day 332...Beyond Grunt

Thursday's hobby day at school, so we troop to the auditorium last period to see the exhibits. There's some hand-carved dinosaurs and a cool model Porsche with racing stripes.

Near the back are two birdhouses made of wood, the pieces evenly matched, all the edges sandpapered smooth. They have wooden pegs instead of nails, and they look like they'll last forever. I read the name on the tag and nearly fall over. Hector Baldwin.

There's only one Hector Baldwin in school, and he lives in Ratchet.

Someone jostles me, and I move along. The bell rings before I've seen everything, so I have to run for the bus.

I'm behind Marty and Hud in the lineup. They're singing in silly high voices, "Houses for tweety-birds, cute yellow tweety-birds…"

Hector's sitting at the front of the bus. His face is bright red, and he looks as though he might cry.

Hud puts his fingers to his cheeks like they're whiskers and waggles them. "I tought I taw a puddy tat…"

That does it. "I'd like to see *you* make a birdhouse!"

I can't believe I just said that.

Hud turns around on the step, squinting down at me. "What'd you say?"

"You didn't enter the hobby show because you're too dumb to make anything."

Hud grabs me by the hair and yanks. I punch him in the gut as hard as I can. Grinning, he jams my fingers against the metal frame of the door. Mr. Murphy says, "Go sit down, Hud."

Hud gives my fingers one last squeeze, and that's when I see Mr. Murphy is out of his seat. He's got gray hair, but he lifts weights at the athletic club in St. Fabien and teaches karate. You don't want to mess with Mr. Murphy.

Hud clumps to the back of the bus. I sit down at the front, sticking my fingers in my pocket. Hector's face is pressed into the windowpane, the tips of his ears red. The bus heads out and does its usual stops in Long Bight and Fiddlers Cove. As Hud walks past, he mutters, "I'll catch up with you later, runt."

There's a stone in my gut, the same one that's there at recess when I'm playing ball hockey by myself or just standing by the fence. Even knowing I got one good punch in doesn't help.

We come to Ratchet. Hector gets out first. He still hasn't looked my way. When we come to Prinny's place, she smiles at me, a sunny-Saturday-morning smile. As the door swings shut, Mr. Murphy says, "Ask your dad about karate lessons, Travis. We teach beginners in St. Fabien two nights a week."

He's only trying to help. But with the cats and hockey, there's no time for karate. "Thanks," I say, and run for the house.

Rayleen's watching the soaps. "I made more brownies," she says. "In the blue tin on the counter."

"They're great," I say. I wish I could tell her how Prinny licked every last bit of icing off her fingers. I eat one fast and call out, "I'm going over to Hector's."

There. I've said it. Too late to change my mind.

～

Hector lives in a house with green siding. Two rows of shrubs pruned like soccer balls lead to the front door. His mother answers the doorbell; she's wearing a flowered dress and sparkly earrings. I ask if Hector's home.

"Please come in," she says. "Hector! You have a visitor. And what's your name, dearie?"

"Travis Keating."

"The doctor's son. How nice."

Hector's standing in the doorway. His cheeks have gone red again. "Want to come for a bike ride?" I say.

"How kind," says Hector's mum. "Now put up your hood, Hector, and don't forget your gloves. Supper's at five forty-five, so don't be late. And make sure you ride facing the traffic. Watch out for Riley's fence—it's too close to the road. I don't know what that man was thinking of. Travis, dearie, are you a responsible bike rider?"

"Yes," I say. She's got more rules than Dad.

Hector pulls up his hood, puts on gloves, and we go outdoors. His mother's still talking as he closes the door. "Let's go up the hill," I say.

His bike looks like it's never been used. We drive up the hill until we get away from all the other houses, then I signal him to stop. He's breathing hard. The only other sounds are the wind coming across the barrens and the squawk of a raven.

"Hector, can you keep a secret?" Could anyone keep a secret from his mum? She'd wear you down like waves wear the rocks smooth.

"I guess," he says.

"*I guess* isn't good enough. Yes or no."

"What sort of secret?"

"One that'll get me in trouble if you rat on me."

"With your father?" Hector asks.

"My father and Rayleen. I don't want Hud finding out either."

"I'll keep it."

I'm pushing my luck. First Abe, then Prinny, and now Hector. "Will you come to Gulley Cove and take the padlock off a fish shack? The screws are stuck. You could saw a hole in the wall, too."

"Why?"

"Will you do it?"

"I'm not allowed to go to Gulley Cove."

"Me neither," I say. "That's why it's a secret."

"Mum says it's not safe there."

"So does Dad."

His face isn't giving anything away. I've blown it, telling him as much as I have. He'll go home and tell his mother, and she'll get on the phone to Dad faster than you can say *cat*.

"Why'd you ask *me*?" he says finally.

"Your birdhouses are so neat. You could saw a hole in a wall easy."

"What's the hole for?"

I take a deep breath. "The cove's not haunted," I say and explain about the cats and the leaking roofs and Blackie's kittens. "If you take off on your bike after school, do you have to tell your mum where you're going?"

"Dunno. Never take off. We could get the saw now. How far to Gulley Cove?"

It's the most he's ever talked. Not that he'd get much chance to open his mouth when his mum was around. "Ten minutes on our bikes."

"What kind of screws?"

"Round ones. All rusty."

"Phillips or Robertson?"

"I don't know," I say. Somehow he's gone from being the nerdy kid at the front of the bus to the expert. "You know anything about cats?"

"Mum won't let me have pets. Too messy."

That figures. "We gotta hustle—I have to feed the cats, and Dad grounded me last week because I was out too late."

Hector uses the back door of his house to get the saw and a screwdriver. When we reach the cove, it takes him two minutes to take the padlock off the first shack.

"Break and enter," he says as we walk inside.

"We could go to the slammer for that."

Hector nods, "Making a hole in a wall—that's vandalism."

Dad doesn't have a rule about vandalism. Yet. "If they put us in the same cell, you can teach me how to make those wooden pegs."

"Shack belongs to my uncle," he says. "Never comes here. Mostly snow's from the nor'east. I'll cut the hole in the lee."

I feel stupid again, not knowing about the winds. Hector says, sawing away, "You gonna feed the cats all winter?"

"Guess so. Else they'll starve."

Hector lays the cut boards neatly on the floor. The sawdust smells nice and the hole's just the right size for Blackie. "What else?" he says.

"Blackie needs a shelter so she can have her kittens."

"Nothing to it—I got wood at home. If anyone asks, we're building a fort, right?"

"Building something isn't vandalism."

"Improving property," he says.

After we fill all the bowls, we bike home fast so his mum won't get upset. "Tomorrow?" Hector asks.

My first hockey practice is tomorrow at five. But if we don't build the shelter soon, I'm worried Blackie will have her kittens outside and I'll never find them.

"Tomorrow's good," I say, wondering if I'll ever make it to the rink. "I'll come to your place to help with the wood. We'll say the fort's on the barrens behind my place."

"See you."

❧

So on Friday, Hector builds a shelter for Blackie inside the first shack. It's a small square box with a roof, insulated with Styrofoam. Hector doesn't need to say much because his hands do the talking, moving slow and careful, never making a mistake.

I've stolen a bath towel from home. I figure stealing for a good cause doesn't really break Rule #1, just puts a kink in it.

When Hector's done, he folds the towel and lays it inside the box. We put food and water dishes near the box, then we sit back on our heels and smile at each other.

"I hope Blackie likes it," I say. "We better head home before it gets dark."

Hector grunts. He can pack a lot of information into a grunt. This one sounds satisfied. I feel good, too, because now I can call on Hector as well as Prinny for help with the cats. Takes some of the weight off.

By the time we bike up the hill to Abe's place, Hector's puffing and blowing. But he doesn't once complain. When we come to my house, he waves good-bye and keeps going.

Nineteen

Days 330 and 329...Stone and Ice

Dad wants me to go shopping in St. Fabien with him Saturday morning before we go to the rink, so I run over to Prinny's place early to fix up a time for Sunday. She must have seen me coming because she's waiting on the front step. Her hair's not as shiny and she's shivering in her T-shirt. I explain about today. Scuffing at the step with her slipper, she says, "Ma's acting up and Da's in a state. So I don't know if I can feed the cats today. I'll try."

"They'll be okay until tomorrow."

"I likes feeding them. But if I'm not at your place tomorrow by one-thirty, you better go without me."

I get that stone-in-my-gut feeling again. Trying to make her smile, I describe the shelter Hector built. "Wait till you see it; it's neat."

"If you got Hector, you don't need me."

"Sure I do. Every weekend."

"I can't build stuff."

She looks like she's going to cry. I say, kind of frantic, "You're loaning me snowshoes. I couldn't go to the cove without them."

Inside the house I hear a sound like a plate smashing on the floor. Prinny flinches. "I gotta go," she says, backs into the house, and closes the door.

If Mum was alive, she'd know what to say to Prinny. Mum could make friends with anyone, from the dog-catcher to the premier.

If Mum was alive, I wouldn't know Prinny.

❧

The dressing room at the rink is just the same as the one in St. John's. Chipped blue paint, black rubber mats on the floor, and stale sweat. Although Cole says hi, no one else talks to me while I put my gear on. But I'm used to being ignored, and it feels great to be on the ice again.

The coach's name is Tony Baldwin, and ten minutes into the practice I know he's going to be okay. Tough, but he can raise a laugh. We do drills for half an hour, then we have a game. I pull my usual tricks and score four goals. Dead silence for the first one, some shifting and mumbling for the second, a feeble yell for the third, and a couple of cheers for the fourth. The guys are looking at me sideways, like they missed something.

Okay by me.

When I come out of the locker room, Dad's waiting. Hud's standing by the boards with a bag of gear, staring at me. I don't know if he watched me score those goals.

I walk past him as if I've never seen him before.

❧

I'm in an igloo built of Styrofoam blocks, and Felix is screaming outside. A polar bear's got him. I gotta save him. But there's no door to the igloo. When I punch the wall, my fist sinks in and the wall closes around it like thick, white glue.

The screaming stops.

With a jolt I wake up. Early Sunday morning, heart hammering, and my hands ice-cold. I drag the blankets over my head and try to go back to sleep.

Grady calls later that morning. I haven't told him about the cats or about not having any friends. So after I talk about the goals I scored, there's not much to say.

That afternoon Prinny doesn't show up. At one-thirty I tell Dad I'm going over to her place so we can go snowshoeing. "Stay in sight of the houses," he says, "and don't be late home. Got that?"

I knock on Prinny's door. Even though it's shut tight, I can hear the radio blaring. No one comes. I bang again and call Prinny's name.

Her father flings the door open. He's wearing overalls and the T-shirt with the burn holes.

"She ain't coming out today," he says and slams the door so hard the windowpanes rattle on the porch.

The door needs painting. The whole house needs painting.

I creep past the kitchen window to the rooms at the back and peer in the first one. A double bed, the sheets all messy, and a wine bottle lying on a chair in a puddle of red.

The next window's Prinny's room. Her door's shut and she's propped up in bed with a book resting on her knees. But she's not reading. She's crying.

I sink down out of sight. I could run home and forget I saw her. She'd never know the difference.

Just like I ran away from the cats at Gulley Cove.

I stand up and tap on the window. Prinny jumps and looks over. Then she scrambles off the bed, scrubs her face with a corner of the quilt, and pushes the window up.

"What's wrong?" I say. "Why can't you come out?"

Her face crumples. "Da kicked Ma out last night."

I gape at her through the tiny squares in the screen. "Was she drunk?"

Prinny nods, picks up a balled-up mass of Kleenex from the bed, and snivels into it. "He won't tell me where she is. At one of her drinking buddies, maybe. Or else at Aunt Ida's in Fiddlers Cove—although she's got pitiful little patience with Ma."

"Did your dad hit you?"

It's her turn to gape at me. "*Da*? Only thing he ever swats is moose flies. Why'd you ask?"

"The way he slammed the door on me, I guess."

"They had a big fight in the middle of the night. She fired a beer bottle at him and broke the screen on the TV. Da loves his TV—that's when he lost his cool." Prinny starts crying again. "Drove off with her. Didn't even let her take a proper jacket."

I truly hate it when a girl cries. "I could ask Dad; maybe he can find out where your mother went."

"Oh…you'd do that for me?"

"Of course I would."

"That's real nice of you." She blows her nose. "You better not knock on the door again, though. Not today. If I'm cooking supper, shove a note through my window."

She looks a little better. I promise I'll ask Dad right away and say good-bye.

There's more than one way to lose your mum, and Prinny's way stinks, too.

Back home, Dad's reading the sports section because it's half-time. I tell him what happened to Prinny's mother. "Can you find out where she is?"

He folds the paper. "Is Prinny all right?"

"She's crying a lot."

"I'll try Ida Quinn in Fiddlers Cove."

After looking in the phone book, he punches the numbers in. "Ida? Dr. Keating here. I wondered if Wilma's with you?…She is?…No, Prinny didn't know where she was…I see…Thanks."

He puts down the phone. "She's at Ida's. She says she's never going home."

"But she's okay?"

"She's an alcoholic, Travis. Once she starts drinking, she can't stop. Until she decides to quit, she won't be okay, no."

That's typical of Dad—he tells it how it is, even though sometimes you wish he wouldn't.

All of a sudden, I'm back in our house in St. John's. Late summer, the petunias all straggly, and he's telling me Mum isn't ever going to get better.

So he *did* warn me. Weird how I'd forgotten that.

"I didn't mean to upset you," Dad says.

"I'd better go tell Prinny where her mother is."

"Do you want me to go with you?"

I sure do. "Nope, it's okay."

A few minutes later, I'm tramping through the snow behind Prinny's house. She's still in her bedroom, and she's wedged the screen up. When she sees me, she opens the window.

"Your mother's at your aunt's," I say.

"When'll she be home?"

"Sounds like she's mad at your dad…once she cools down, I expect she'll come back."

"You telling me she's gone for good?"

It doesn't seem like the time to lie. "That's what she said."

"There's been lots of days I wished she'd go live someplace else." Prinny starts to cry again. "Now she has."

"It's not your fault!"

"I used to yell at her something awful. But now alls I want is for her to come home. So what if she's a lousy mother? She's still my ma."

Another thing I hate is not knowing what to do. Then I remember the tinfoil package in my pocket. Pushing it through the window, I say, "Rayleen made these. Brownies, like the one you had at Gulley Cove."

She blows her nose again. "Thanks."

"Can you come to the cove next weekend?"

"I'll have to see if Da's settled by then." She's playing with the catch on the screen. "You better go."

I run down the driveway, hoping Aunt Ida will get in a big fight with Prinny's mother and send her straight home. Then I get an idea. One day soon, I'll ask Prinny for dinner at our place after school. Her dad can cook his own dinner for once; and we can keep quiet about the cats in front of my dad for the space of an hour or so.

Rayleen'll come up with something better than canned beans.

I tell Dad what happened, then say I'm going snow-shoeing for a while. When I sneak out to Gulley Cove, Rocky actually comes in to eat while I'm sitting on the coil of rope.

Makes my day.

Makes Dad's day when I get home twenty minutes early.

Twenty

Day 328...Hud. Again.

On Monday, Prinny's on the bus, but her hair's a mess. Mrs. Dooks starts the week by springing a social studies test on us. Third period, I realize my English text is in my locker and she tells me to get it.

I'm twirling the numbers on the lock when a voice says, "Well, lookit who's here."

I'd know that voice anywhere. I pivot, my eyes darting this way and that. No one else in sight.

Pushing off from the locker, I duck under Hud's arm. But he's too quick for me. He grabs me, throws me against the metal door, and clamps me there.

"Gotcha," he says. "You made a right idjit out of me on the bus. How about telling me you're sorry?"

I open my mouth to say *I'm sorry*. "I'm not sorry" is what comes out. From me, the champion liar.

"Guess I'll have to make you sorry," he says. He's

got a zit on his chin, a yellowing bruise under his ear, and he's smiling like I just gave him fifty bucks.

Funeral Face. No-brainer.

He punches me hard in the chest. Twice. I double over, terrified I'm going to barf all over his sneakers.

"Lots more where that come from," he says and strolls off down the corridor.

My legs are wobbling like I just did drills for two hours straight. I lean against the locker, fighting for breath, a roaring in my ears.

If I don't get out of here, Mrs. Dooks will make me write an essay on tardiness, another of her favorite topics. Slowly I straighten, trying to take deeper breaths. I find my English text and shuffle back to class. Mrs. Dooks gives me a sharp look, then tells Stevie he'd better smarten up or he'll fail next week's test.

Whenever Hud gets ahold of me, it's as if I'm on the rink with the bleachers full and suddenly realize I'm wearing nothing but skates and a helmet. Weird how humiliation's worse than pain.

❧

As we're finishing drills at the rink that evening, me moving in slow gear, Hud takes a seat in the bleachers, his hockey bag beside him. Bantams have ice time right after us. He's probably hoping I'm crippled from the basting he gave me.

I'll show him. Cole and Stevie are both forwards; we pass the puck back and forth, and I score three goals with two assists. Tonight the guys on our team cheer right away, and Cole high-fives me.

Even though my ribs hurt like crazy, it feels great. Like I'm back with the St. John's Jets.

I act like I never saw Hud.

Twenty-one

Day 327...Kit Kat

When I get up the next morning, it looks as though it snowed most of the night. So I head over to Abe's place early. My chest feels like I was trampled by a herd of caribou.

Lucy comes running to say hello. When I bend to pat her, it hurts. Hurts worse to shovel. But finally the path and the steps are clear. Abe opens the door and inspects the job.

"You're slow today. Right logy." He's frowning. "Your dad find out about you and them cats?"

I almost drop the shovel. He thinks Dad gave me a beating for going to Gulley Cove. "Hud got me against the locker door," I say, wondering why it should be so easy to tell Abe when I'm not going to tell Dad.

No point expecting Dad to fix anything.

"I might be an old guy, but I could teach you a turn-up or two for the likes of Hud Quinn," Abe says. He fumbles in the pocket of his overalls. "Found this," he adds gruffly, and hands over a Kit Kat bar.

"Thanks!"

"You want to work off them boards quicker, you can shovel to the barn another time."

"If you show me those knots."

"You nag worse'n a woman."

I pat Lucy, say good-bye through a mouthful of chocolate, and head home. Wonder of wonders. Abe gave me a present.

More wonders are waiting at school. At lunchtime, Cole, Buck, and Stevie all kid around with me while we're standing in line at the canteen; then Cole sits next to me on the bus on the way home. Nothing like scoring a few goals to make the experiment look up. I might even get to like living in Ratchet.

So I'm feeling pretty good when I snowshoe to the cove after school. Blackie's not in her box, but the food's nearly all gone, so I fill the bowl.

Felix and I meet up in the fourth shack. Although he does his routine hissing and growling, he lets me sit near him while he washes his face. I ramble on about Prinny's ma, Hud and my sore ribs, Hector who grunts, and his mother who never shuts up. "There sure is more to talk about since I met you guys," I tell Felix.

For a moment I swear he looks smug.

Twenty-two

Day 326...Felix

Wednesday after school, I snowshoe the shortcut. It feels safer than the track.

I can hear the noise before I reach the last hill down to the cove. A flock of ravens are diving and swooping over the fish shacks, making a big racket. I get this uneasy feeling, like I should hurry, and I take the hill as fast as I can.

Near the trees, a dark smudge is lying on the snow. My heart starts banging away; the whole time I'm hurrying toward it, I'm wanting to run the other way. Blood's spattered on the snow, so red it looks like fresh paint. The smudge is a cat, a ginger cat.

Felix...

It's not Felix; it's the little ginger cat I never got around to naming. It's dead, neck twisted, a trickle of dried blood on its jaw.

Big paw prints have packed down the snow, some of them stained with blood. My eyes skitter among the trees. There aren't any wolves left in Newfoundland, Mrs. Dooks said. And coyotes don't usually make it this far north. Anyway, they'd have eaten the cat.

Dogs. The same pack that chased the caribou.

I don't want to meet up with a pack of bloodthirsty dogs, not on my own, way down here at the cove. But leaving the ginger cat to be ripped to pieces by the ravens isn't on.

The box of cat food in my pack is in a plastic bag. I take the bag out and tug off my mittens. Clenching my teeth, I wrap the cat in the bag. Its legs have gone stiff, like they're frozen solid. One of the ravens dive-bombs me, so close I can hear the wind swish through its feathers. I duck, covering my head.

"Quark, quark! Quark!"

That's when I notice smaller paw prints, spotted with blood, leading from near the dead cat into the rocks. Cat prints.

Oh man, I don't like this. I tug at the rubber bindings and take Prinny's snowshoes off. Carrying the plastic bag, ravens screaming overhead, I crouch down under the boughs and follow the prints to a gap between two rocks.

Felix is lying there under the overhang. His eyes are shut. There's a big slice in his shoulder, the fur flapped open to show muscle and bone. He's bled lots and it's gone sticky on his fur.

The wind off the sea cuts through my fleece like it's made of paper. I lean over the nearest rock and vomit.

I wish it wasn't Felix. I wish I could turn the clock back so everything was still okay.

Throwing up always makes me feel like pond slime. I scour my mouth with snow crystals to get rid of the taste, trying so hard not to look at Felix that all I can do is look at him.

His ribs give a little heave. Up, then down. My heart leaps in my chest.

He does it again—up, then down.

He's alive.

I gotta get him to the vet.

Trying to think rather than act, I sit back on my haunches. If I take him to the vet and he's got feline leukemia, his life's not worth a flea egg. Dr. Larkin'll put him to sleep. But if I don't take him, odds are he'll die anyway.

I'm between a rock and a hard place. Between two rocks, actually—one slathered with puke.

I leave Felix and the dead cat under the overhang. Moving fast, I fill all the bowls , stopping between each shack to yell and wave my arms at the ravens. Maybe the cat food was what brought the dogs to Gulley Cove; dogs can smell food a long way off.

Blackie's waiting for me inside the first shack. I want to pick her up and hug her, I'm so happy to see her. "I'll be back tomorrow," I say. "Stay inside if the dogs come back. The opening Hector made is too small for them to get through, and you'll be safe."

Back at the rocks, I lift Felix onto the snow, glad he's unconscious because he'd never let me pick him up otherwise. Then I wrap him in my sweater. He's heavier than I expected, his body limp. A couple of fleas hop from his fur to my hands. After I pick them off, I push the dead cat farther back under the overhang where the ravens can't get it, and cover it with snow.

I lower Felix into my pack, leaving an opening at the top so he can breathe. Then I put the snowshoes on and settle the pack against my chest, like those baby carriers mothers wear.

Trying to jog without bouncing Felix around in the pack, I take off up the slope. By the time I stagger up the last hill to Abe's, it feels like I've run the Boston Marathon.

I'm wheezing for air as I knock on his door. "You come to shovel the barn?" he says. Then he looks closer. "What's wrong, b'y? You're all a-bivver."

"Can you take me to St. Fabien in your truck? One of the cats is in my bag. Hurt bad."

"Truck's got a flat," Abe says. "Who hurt the cat?"

"Must've been a pack of dogs—they killed another cat." I give this sound midway between a gasp and a groan. "I better go. Maybe Rayleen can get her husband's truck."

"You go on home. I'll call her on the telephone, light a bonfire under her."

Now that I've stopped, I'm not sure I can walk another step. Trying to drag some air down my throat, my ribs paining like Hud just beat up on me again, I head down the path to the gate.

Rayleen's waiting in her driveway behind the wheel of her husband's half-ton, the engine running. She leans over and opens the door. "Move it."

The step feels a hundred feet tall. I climb in, pull the door shut, and rest the pack on my lap.

"Seat belt," Rayleen says, backing out and turning with a screech of tires. "We're off to St. Fabien. I phoned the vet clinic, told them it was an emergency."

She's liking this. More exciting than the soaps.

She's got the heat on high; on the radio, Shania Twain's singing about a party. When I open the zipper again and push the sweater back, Felix's ribs are still moving up and down. I hug the pack to my chest.

"Where'd you find the cat?" Rayleen says.

"Out on the barrens." Then I remember Abe phoned her. "Behind Abe's place."

She peers in the bag, one hand on the wheel. "Wouldn't win no beauty contests."

"It's a stray. Dogs must've hurt it."

She's belting down the highway, humming along with Shania. At the end of the song, she says, "I called your dad. He'll meet you at the vet's after work."

I huddle down, clutching Felix like I expect him to save my life, not the other way around.

Dr. Larkin's waiting for us. "Hello, Travis," she says, really friendly. "Let's take the cat into the examining room."

"I'll be off, then," Rayleen says. She winks at me. "You ask the vet if that ain't the homeliest critter she's ever seen."

The vet goes into the same room we were in before, lifts Felix out of the bag, and lays him on the table. "He's certainly not starving," she says. "You've done a good job."

She pulls the fur back from his teeth, checking his gums. "He's lost some blood—not too much, though. I'll have to anaesthetize him and stitch him up."

"What if he's got that disease?"

"Feline leukemia? I'll test for that, of course. But first we have to—"

"When will you know if he's got it? Because you're going to kill him if he does."

"I won't do anything like that without talking to you first about all the options," she says. "You've got to trust me."

She's nailed the problem right there. There's trust you don't know you have until it gets broken; and there's trust you gotta build from the ground up.

"Does the cat have a name?" she asks.

"Felix. After the goalie."

"Felix Potvin? Good name." She smiles at me, and even though I'm worried sick about Felix, I can't help smiling back. Then she says, "You're going to tell me where the other cats are, right?"

"Wasn't planning on it."

"Winter's coming on, Travis. If any of the cats have feline leukemia, they'll suffer terribly." She reaches into her pile of pamphlets, pulls one out and sticks a photo of a sick cat under my nose.

Skin and bones... "No fair, showing me that!"

"It's not fair the cats were abandoned."

I try for Funeral Face, but Felix's paw prints, little red splodges in the snow, keep getting in the way. The words push themselves up from somewhere so deep I can't stop them. "Even though my mum was sick, she liked being alive—why would cats be any different?"

"Oh," says Dr. Larkin, her voice gone quiet. "Oh. I see."

"No, you don't."

She sits down so her eyes are on a level with mine. It's like she's searching for what to say. "Do you know why I wanted to be a vet? Because animals can't tell us what's wrong or ask for help...right now I'm trying to speak for all the cats you've been looking after."

She's backed me into the fence, like Hud. "If you tell Dad about the other cats, I'll be in big trouble."

"Then he can't be much of a father," she says. "I think you'd better tell him the truth."

"Easy for you to say."

"Think about it." She stands up. "I'll get my assistant and we'll operate on Felix right away—I'll let you know how he is as soon as I can."

"Can you fix him up?" I blurt. "For sure?"

"I can't guarantee it, but I'll do my best."

I sit down in the waiting room where I can watch the parking lot. I trusted Dad to do his best with Mum and look what happened. Why would I trust a vet with crazy orange hair?

I'm responsible for those cats. If I blow it, I don't know that I can handle the guilt.

For the first time, I wonder if Dad ever feels guilty.

Think Before You Act. I take a stub of pencil out of my pocket, pick up a kid's coloring book from the table, find a clean page and start writing.

(1) If the cats have feline leukemia, they'll die
　(a) at Dr. Larkin's if I tell her about Gulley Cove,
　(b) in the snow and ice at the cove if I don't.
(2) If the cats don't have feline leukemia, it's okay
　to tell her. She might help me protect them
　from the dogs, too.
(3) Either way, I'm in trouble with Dad because
　I'm running out of lies.

Then I sit back and look at what I've written. An awful lot of *ifs* and no way of knowing the truth.

Skin and bones… The last few times I visited Mum in the hospital, her skin was yellow and her eyes were sunk in her head, like it was getting ready to be a skull. One evening, she told Dad she was hurting all over, her fingernails digging little grooves in the sheet. Dad went to the nursing station and from down the corridor I could hear his don't-argue-with-me voice. A couple of minutes later, a nurse gave Mum a needle, and I watched her slowly relax until she was able to smile at me and ask about my new Bauer skates.

Skin and bones… Felix's sore eye. Blackie's matted fur. Ghost's ribs sticking out. There aren't any painkillers at Gulley Cove.

No *if* about that.

Twenty-three

Day 326...Secrets and Lies

Half an hour later the Toyota pulls up and Dad gets out. He walks in, his hair ruffled by the wind, and sits down next to me. "What's up, Travis?"

"I brought in a cat who was attacked by dogs—I guess it was dogs. The vet's operating on him now."

"Did you find the cat out on the barrens?"

"Yes," I say, stretching the truth like a rubber band.

"Whereabouts?"

"I'll tell you later."

"Have you had supper?"

"I'm not hungry."

He puts an arm around my shoulders and keeps it there until Dr. Larkin comes into the waiting room in her white coat. She nods at me and Dad.

"Could you come into the examining room?"

When she's closed the door, I say, "This is my dad. How's Felix?"

"Chip Keating," Dad says and they shake hands.

Dr. Larkin looks at me, smiling. "Good news. The feline leukemia test was negative. I stitched Felix's shoulder, neutered him, and cleaned up his eye infection. We gave him a flea and ear-mite treatment as well. He's a tough old cat—probably nine or ten years old—so he'll be fine."

I suck a deep breath past the tightness in my chest, relief tasting better than a hundred Kit Kat bars. Then I say, "The dogs killed one of the other cats."

She bites her lip. "Will you take me to see them sometime soon?"

"Yeah." Decision made.

"How about Saturday afternoon?"

"I get home from hockey about twelve-thirty," I say, and tell her where we live. All this time Dad hasn't said a word.

She says to him, "You're the new doctor, aren't you?"

"We moved here in October from St. John's—a big change for both of us."

"It hasn't taken Travis long to find a place where he can help out," she says. "I'll drop by around two on Saturday, and we'll check the rest of the colony."

A whole colony of cats is news to Dad. He doesn't

even blink. "I'm off on Saturday, so I'll go with you…How much do we owe you for today?"

"Why don't we wait until I see the rest of the cats? Our clinic has special rates for feral animals," she says. "See you both on Saturday."

Dad and I walk out to the Toyota. Once he pulls onto the road, he says, "We'll discuss all this when we get home."

I try and do the monk thing, sitting still in the Toyota and waiting. Waiting's my least favorite occupation. So then I try and work out what to say so Dad won't totally lose his cool.

We get home and go indoors. Dad sits down on the couch and I take the chair across from him.

"Okay, Travis, come clean."

The plan was to edge into what's been going on— how I saved Felix's life and how feeding the other cats is making their lives better. But telling Dr. Larkin about them was such a big deal that caution and common-sense have gone down the tubes. Anger's burning my throat like when you eat extra-hot salsa.

"I went to Gulley Cove," I say, "and found these starving cats. So I've been feeding them for over a month. Lying to you and Rayleen."

"Rayleen told you not to go to Gulley Cove."

"I went anyway."

"Why?"

"I didn't have any friends here—no one was talking to me on the bus or at school because I'm from away and I don't fit in. What was I supposed to do? Ride my bike up and down the street every day?"

"That's why I wanted us to move to St. Fabien."

"I'd still be a townie!"

Dad undoes the top button of his shirt like his collar's too tight. "So our experiment's been a failure—you lied about that as well."

"Not since I found the cats, it hasn't been. They gave me something to do."

"But you still miss St. John's."

"St. John's and Grady—even our garden."

"Did you really scrape your hand on the rocks near Abe's? Or was it at Gulley Cove?"

"I didn't scrape it at all. Felix scratched me."

"That's a lot of lies."

"At first I didn't want to be bothered with the cats. But when I saw what shape they were in, I couldn't just leave them to starve. You wouldn't walk away if someone was hurt on the street."

"So the day of the blizzard you were coming back from Gulley Cove. And of course you didn't want to move to St. Fabien, because of the cats. Travis, you should have told me!"

"I liked it being my secret. The cats were the only ones who made me feel I belonged here."

"But I might have been able to help."

"I got help anyway. From Prinny and Hector. Abe, too. He gave me some boards to fix the wharf where the wood's rotten."

Dad winces. "You could have fallen into the sea— which is why I made the rule about Gulley Cove in the first place."

"I hate all these rules you keep making! Don't do this, don't do that. I'm nearly twelve years old. You treat me like I'm in kindergarten."

Dad goes quiet, like Dr. Larkin. Then he says, "I couldn't bear for anything to happen to you, not after losing your mother. That's why I make so many rules."

Losing Mum? Like she was a library book he put down somewhere or a pen that's gone missing?

"The fishermen left the cats to starve," I say, "but I'm not going to. I'm not staying away from Gulley Cove. I don't care what you say!"

He's staring at the carpet. The kitchen clock's ticking away, the wind's whining around the corner of the house, and inside me the volcano's bubbling. I wait for him to ground me again, or put hockey off-limits.

"Tell me about the cats," he says finally. "How many are there?"

"Only if you promise I can still look after them."

"I won't make you abandon them," he says. "How did you find out about them?"

I start slow, with the kids on the bus talking about ghosts. But then the words pour out about Abe and Lucy, Prinny and Hector, Felix, Blackie, Ghost, and Rocky. Last of all, I tell him about the little ginger cat that I never named.

Dad pats me on the shoulder, kind of awkward. "I'm proud of you, son."

"You *are?* Even though I told all those lies?"

"You did what you thought was right, and it hasn't been easy."

"Oh." I'll never figure out grown-ups. Specially Dad. *Proud* of me?

I say eagerly, "I want to keep Felix and tame him, and I have to find homes for Blackie and her kittens. Then there's the rest of them—they can't stay there all winter, not with those dogs around."

Dad's frowning, like he does when he's thinking hard. "I'm trying to work out how you can go to the cove without me worrying myself to death," he says. "A cell phone might be the answer—you'd still be in range of the tower at St. Fabien. If I buy you one, will you promise to use it only at the cove, and only for emergencies?" He tugs his ear. "New rule. Sorry about that."

"Wow, that'd be neat."

"I have to be able to trust you, though. That's the trouble with telling lies; it means I don't know whether I can believe you anymore. So no more lying."

He means it. Big time. "Okay."

Then he gets me in a headlock and we end up wrestling on the floor. After that, we heat up the beef stew Rayleen left on the stove, and eat it with big chunks of homemade bread.

Twenty-four

Day 325...New Boarder

The next afternoon, Hector and me go to Gulley Cove. Fresh snow's covered up the dog tracks and the blood. Blackie's not in the box Hector made, but the towel's packed down in a circle with a few black hairs sticking to it, so she's probably been sleeping there.

We decide the best thing for the little ginger cat is a burial at sea. Using an old rope, we lower the cat from the end of the wharf. Hector's mother takes him to funerals in St. Fabien, so he repeats parts of the service in a solemn voice, speaking slow, like it's important.

In a weird way, even though it reminds me of Mum's funeral, I feel better after that. As we're coiling up the wet rope, I say, "We gotta work on your mum so you can have one of Blackie's kittens."

He looks doubtful. "Don't reckon Dad would mind. But Mum...my older brothers weren't allowed even a goldfish. They both live in St. John's now, and they both own dogs. Big dogs that track mud in the house and pee on the front steps."

Four whole sentences out of Hector. Amazing. "We'll have to get your dad on our side first."

Hector grunts, a disbelieving grunt. We hurry home because Dad's picking Felix up after work. When I first moved here, time moved really slow. Now there's so much to do I can't fit it all in.

It feels okay to have Dad's help.

The back room is where he piled everything he couldn't find a place for. I pack the boxes against the wall, carve an opening in an empty one, take a sheet out of the cupboard, and fix a bed inside the box. After setting out food and water, I run to Baldwin's Store for cat litter, which I pour into a washbasin with newspaper under it. I hope Felix figures out what it's for.

I hope he doesn't tear the room apart looking for a way out.

Dad brings him home in a plastic carrier, Felix howling like he lost his best friend. "*Aaaiiiieeeooww...*" I lift the flap and latch it to the top of the carrier, but Felix doesn't budge. His shoulder's been shaved. A row of stitches curves across it, knotted like the ones on Frankenstein's monster.

I leave him alone and go for supper. When I come back, he's sitting on top of one of the boxes. There's a dent in the cat food, a pile of poop in the litter, and he's down to hissing.

"This is your new home, Felix," I say. "I didn't like it here at first, so it might take you a while to get used to it, too." Then I do my math homework sitting on the floor near the door, talking out loud as I calculate the areas of different triangles. Next I tell him about the Alberta tar sands, and what a *précis* is.

By the time he's tamed, he'll be the best-educated cat in Ratchet.

Twenty-five

Day 324...Cats and Dogs

Soon after lunch on Friday, the school furnace starts belching black smoke into the boiler room. So there's a fire alarm, then we all get sent home early. Fine with me. Gives me time to go to Gulley Cove before hockey. The sun's shining, and I'm in the mood for a change; so I walk the highway, planning to snowshoe the road along the cliffs. The sea's glittering like thousands of strobe lights. At the last house before Abe's, sheets are billowing on the line like blue sails.

A snowmobile's coming up behind me and I move to the side of the road, wondering what Dr. Larkin'll think of Gulley Cove. Wondering if any of the other cats have feline leukemia.

The snowmobile stops alongside me. Hud gets off.

He tugs off his helmet and lays it on the seat. "Fancy meeting you here," he says. "Right little show-off, you are, scoring all them goals."

I grip the edges of the snowshoes, fear rising in my throat until I almost gag. He kicks out so fast I don't see it coming. Pain flashes through my kneecap as if he's stabbed me. I stagger sideways. He grabs one snowshoe, throwing it on the bank.

I shove the point of the other one into his belly. He gives this surprised squawk, like a raven. Then he lets out a string of curses, seizes me by the right arm so I lose my footing, and bends my wrist backward.

I let out a thin, high scream, waiting for the bones to crack. Hud's whole weight's on my wrist and he's snarling like a wild animal. The snowbanks whirl around and I'm still screaming…and then he lets go.

I land on one shoulder, trying to shield my wrist. "No more goals for you, buddy," Hud says. "Not this week, anyway."

The snowmobile roars to life. He swirls in a tight circle and takes off toward the community.

Somewhere out on the barrens, a real raven squawks.

❧

I'm not crying. Ice from the road is melting against my cheek, that's all. Crying would be one step beyond humiliation.

Very carefully I edge my sleeve up and lay my wrist against the ice until the pain subsides a little. I gotta move, in case someone comes along. It'd be stupid to get run over.

When I stand up, the horizon stays mostly level. Gingerly I test out my wrist, catching my breath as I try to move my fingers. It isn't broken, so that's something. No use thinking I can stickhandle, though.

All I want to do is go home, crawl under the covers, and stay there the whole weekend. Or the rest of my life. If Felix was a dog, he'd keep me company.

Felix. Blackie.

The dogs.

Supporting the sore wrist in my other hand, I check out the snowshoes. Neither of them's damaged. I can use my left hand to fit the bindings over my boots, and feeding the cats one-handed shouldn't be a problem.

If I go home, Hud wins.

❧

I fill the bowls in the fourth shack first. Rocky and Patches race off into the trees, where I catch a glimpse of the other gray cat. Right away I name it Cloud.

When I go into the first shack, lifting the door so it doesn't scrape on the wharf, I can tell there's a cat inside. I start talking really soft and kneel down so I can see inside Blackie's box. Three wet little kittens are lying on the towel, and she's panting, her eyes wild, as another kitten slides out from under her tail. She reaches round, tears the little sac it's wrapped in, and licks its face. The kitten's slimy, its eyes tight shut, but it's breathing. Then Blackie bites through the cord coming out of the kitten's belly.

She's panting again. I never saw anything get born, so I go a little closer. Blackie doesn't seem to care. But instead of another kitten, a shiny pink lump comes out, like a raw sausage. Blackie sniffs at it, then starts eating it. I look the other way fast, trying not to listen to her chew.

When I look back, she's lying flat as though she's tired out. The newest kitten is wiggling and squirming, trying to get closer to her, and one of the others is glommed to her, sucking away. But two of them aren't moving.

Ready to back off in a flash, I lift one of them and hold it in my left hand. It weighs hardly anything, and it's perfectly made, with tiny claws, and slits for eyes. But it's dead.

I stroke it with the tip of my finger, the pain in my wrist not seeming to matter. It probably died because Blackie didn't have enough to eat before I started feeding her. The other kitten's dead, too. Carefully I lay them both by the door so they're touching each other.

Moving slow and easy like Hector, I nudge the

newest kitten into Blackie's belly. As it burrows into her, she curls her body around it and lifts her head, looking right at me.

"You still have two fine kittens, Blackie. I'm going to phone my dad, and we'll take all three of you home with us. You stay right here, okay?"

She doesn't look like she's going anywhere.

I go outside and use the new cell phone to call Dad at work. I'm in luck because he's between patients. "Dad? Blackie had her kittens, but two of them died. There's two left, though. Can you come here on the snowmobile with the cat carrier, and we'll take her and the kittens home?"

"Are you all right?"

"Yeah…well, mostly."

"I can't get away for at least another hour, Travis. It'll be dark by then—are you wearing warm clothes?"

"My snowmobile suit. I'll wait for you inside the first shack." I don't tell him the dogs are the reason I'll be inside. No sense getting him riled up.

"We can't put her in the same room as Felix."

"She can go in the back porch with the washer and dryer."

"How many of these cats did you say there are?" he asks, not sounding too happy.

"The rest are wilder; they won't let me near them. Don't worry, Dad. I'll find a home for the kittens."

"All right…Hang tough, and I'll be there as soon as I can. Give Rayleen a call so she knows what's up."

I talk to Rayleen and push the End button. Nothing's moving on the barrens. The wind's gone still and the sea's whispering to itself, full of secrets. Dad's a long way away. Even Abe's too far for comfort.

The dogs know the way here. Know about the cats.

I go back inside the shack and sit down. The two kittens are nursing and Blackie's eyes look dark and gentle. Cats can be happy, can't they?

I know what I should do next. But I don't want to.

I pick up the dead kittens. One of them's black and the other one's ginger and white. With their flat little faces and round ears, they look like miniature lion cubs.

"I'm sorry, Blackie," I say. "We can't just leave them here. If we do, they'll get maggots, like that raccoon Grady and me found." Then I go back out again.

Lying down on the boards, I drop the kittens into the sea. They float for a while, bouncing around on top of the swell. But then they sink. I stare down into the water until I can't see them anymore, until they're all mixed up with the rocks on the bottom.

A heavy stick's leaning against the wall in one corner of the shack. I put it nearby, pull the door shut with one hand, and sit down again near Blackie. She and the kittens are asleep, although her ears are twitching like she's listening.

"I bet you'll be a good mum, Blackie," I say, "and you'll like having a real home. My mum loved being home on weekends. One time, she had me slice strawberries, then she covered angel food cake with berries and pink ice cream and invited Grady and his parents over for dessert—she knew them so well that she didn't have to clean the house before they came. She hated vacuuming. I bought her a fridge magnet for Christmas once that said, Vacuuming Sucks." Then I talk about Grady and how we used to play *Mario* and *Blades of Steel* on Game Boy.

It's dark by now and I've run out of things to say. I wish I had a flashlight. A couple of times I'm sure I hear a dog barking, and clutch the stick to my chest.

Noises sound different in the dark. Maybe the dead fishermen come back here at night, too dead to fix their shacks, but alive enough to know that the cod are gone and all their hard work's rotting away.

The tide's rising, waves lapping at the stilts under the shack. Suddenly, over the splash and gurgle of the sea, I hear another sound—a howl that's like Felix with the volume turned up.

The dogs.

I stand up, gripping the stick in my left hand, my nails digging into the wood, and shove the door open with my shoulder. Then I wedge it shut behind me. The sea's black as oil. The barrens come down to meet it, vast and empty, as though they've been there forever. A dog barks from far up the hill, followed by a chorus of *yips* and *yaps*, loud and excited.

By scuffling through the snow with my boots, I uncover some stones on the track and put them in the pocket where I keep my whistle. Then I wait for whatever's going to happen next.

Three dogs come over the crest of the hill. One lifts its muzzle to the sky and bays.

"Go away!" I yell as loud as I can.

The dogs stop, peering down the hill, so I shout some more and whack the stick against a granite boulder. Ghost and the other cats are probably scared witless. But as I back up toward the wharf, the dogs are slithering down the hill, breaking through the crust.

It slows them down. *Hurry up, Dad. Get here fast.*

They're nearly at the bottom of the hill. "Go home! Get out of here!" I take out the whistle and blast it.

They stop in their tracks, looking around as though they're not sure what to do next. The smallest dog, a beagle, sits down, panting. The two big dogs, one black and one tan-colored, make uneasy circles in the snow. A frayed rope's attached to the black dog's collar.

Now what do I do? Throw rocks at them, like Hud?

"Go home, you guys—you shouldn't be here."

The beagle sidles up to me, tail between its legs, and sniffs my boots. As I reach down to pat it on the head, it backs off in a hurry. But then it crawls closer again, and this time stays put. Wondering if I'm nuts, I put the stick down and rub the beagle's ears. It wags its tail, its whole body wriggling with pleasure.

The other two dogs are still pacing back and forth. When I click my fingers at the tan-colored one, it gives a low, warning snarl. The black dog sits down, not too close, head tilted as it watches me and the beagle.

None of the dogs look one bit interested in chasing cats. Maybe they're just playing hooky, having some fun.

The beagle rolls over, its tongue hanging out. I'm scratching its belly when a snowmobile comes over the top of the hill, engine growling, its headlight throwing a bar of light on the snow. The dogs' heads jerk around and the beagle scrambles to its feet. They all turn tail and bolt up the hill, following their own tracks, the beagle last in line.

It better be Dad on the snowmobile. Not Hud.

My body's a dark blob against the white and there's no place to hide. I pick up the stick again. If it's Hud, I'll call 911 on the cell phone.

By now the snowmobile's at the bottom of the hill. It pulls up by the first shack and Dad gets off. As I stumble over to meet him, he flicks on a flashlight.

"You okay, Travis? I've been worried about you. Sorry it took me so long."

"I'm fine."

"Didn't I see dogs running up the hill?" I nod. "The same ones that hurt Felix?"

"I don't think so. They were too friendly."

"Were you planning to use that stick on them?"

"If they got too close to Blackie or any of the other cats, I was."

Dad sighs. His sighs are like Hector's grunts. This one says *Are you out of your mind? A stick against three dogs?*

"Where's Blackie?" he says, untying the cat carrier from the back of the Ski-Doo.

I lead him around to the door of the shack and rest the stick against the wall. But when I pull on the door with my left hand, the wood jams.

As I yank on it, Dad says, "Use both hands."

"I hurt the other one—will you open the door?"

"Did the dogs bite you?" he says urgently, reaching for my right hand. I shake my head, keeping my hand by my side. "How did you hurt it?"

I promised not to lie again. But I'm not going to tell Dad a local bully's haunting me worse than any ghost. "We need to check on Blackie."

Dad pulls the door open and walks into the shack. Blackie meows, short and sharp.

"It's okay," I say, "it's Dad, and we're going to take you home with us."

"After you tell me how you hurt your hand."

"I had a fight with one of the guys at school. He doesn't like me because I'm a townie and I score too many goals."

"What's his name?"

"I can deal with it, Dad!"

"I'll check your hand when we get home," he says in his don't-argue-with-me voice. Then he kneels down near Blackie's box, speaking to her gently, like she's a kid he's giving a needle to. "Travis, help me put her in the carrier. She's used to you."

When we pick up the edges of the towel, she moans and yowls, her eyes going wild again. But she doesn't scratch either of us. By sliding the whole towel into the carrier, we get her in with her kittens and wrap the carrier with a blanket Dad brought with him. Then I climb onto the back seat of the Ski-Doo, the carrier against my jacket, and we drive home.

Blackie goes in the back porch in an empty dresser drawer, on the same towel we brought her in. Although I can tell she's spooked by the new place, she starts right in licking her kittens. Everything taking twice as long with one hand, I feed her, give her water, and set up the kitty litter in Rayleen's mixing bowl because it's the only thing I can find that's big enough.

Dad's in the kitchen. He puts down the potato masher and pushes up my sleeve. My wrist's swollen;

you can still see the marks of Hud's fingers. "From the looks of this, the other guy fought dirty," Dad says. "He hurt you on purpose, didn't he? Who was it?"

"Someone at school—I told you."

"Give me his name and I'll go to the principal. There's only one policy for bullying—zero tolerance."

"If I tell on him, he'll really have it in for me."

"If you let him continue, he'll never learn any better."

"He's not into learning—and it wouldn't have happened if we hadn't moved here!"

"Wherever we live, it's up to me to look after you," Dad says. "That's my job."

"I can look after myself. Supper's getting cold."

"One more sign of trouble and I'll go to the principal regardless."

Dad's pretty good at stubborn mode, too. I stare at the floor. "How long before I can play hockey?"

"A week or so. We'll put some ice on it right away, and I'll make a sling for you."

After we eat, Dad decides I can't do the dishes with one hand. I leave a message at Cole's to tell him why I wasn't at hockey, then go do my homework so it's out of the way. Tonight Felix and me learn about the rivers of India and irregular polygons.

Twenty-six

Day 323...Patience, Praise, and Pudding

When I wake up in the morning, my wrist's twice its normal size. After icing it again, I hide it under a shirt with extra-long sleeves. The coach won't be too pleased I can't play hockey for a week.

I can't quit scoring goals just to keep Hud happy; scoring goals is what I do best. So I'll have to be more careful. Vigilant. Spelled with one *l*.

After breakfast, I find a note from Prinny under the front door. She can't go to Gulley Cove this weekend because her father's cleaning out the shed and needs her help.

I guess her mother didn't come home.

Dr. Larkin arrives prompt at two, carrying a black bag and an animal trap. Her hair's pinned up today, but bits are flying loose. While she's taking off her boots in the porch, I say, "We have three more cats now. Blackie and two kittens."

"You'll have to find a bigger house," she says.

Felix has his usual hissy fit, but she sweet-talks him into letting her check his stitches and his eye. When she puts him down, he scrambles to the tallest box and sits there, tail whipping like a windshield wiper.

She looks at Blackie and the kittens next. "I'll take a blood sample," she says, "and treat her for fleas and ear mites. And I'll give you pills to deworm her."

Blood sample. So much has happened since yesterday that I'd forgotten about feline leukemia.

Not Blackie, I think. Please, not her.

Blackie cowers down, shivering, while Dr. Larkin takes the blood sample from her front leg. The blood gets mixed with some liquid and put into a little white plastic box. Then we have to wait fifteen minutes.

By now I've remembered kittens can catch the disease from their mother, even before they're born.

Dr. Larkin rubs the flea stuff into Blackie's fur, puts her down on the floor and shows me the tablets for the worms, explaining how to use them. Blackie jumps back into the drawer with her kittens, who start nursing. She blinks at me like she doesn't have a worry in the world.

These cats are determined to teach me patience.

I don't remember one word about the worms.

Dad makes tea and brings it in while the vet packs away her gear. I eat one of Rayleen's butterscotch squares without even tasting it. Finally Dr. Larkin checks her watch and picks up the little plastic box.

"Negative," she says. "See?"

"You mean Blackie's *safe*?"

"She doesn't have leukemia. Considering what a rough time she had at the cove, she's in excellent shape. I'd say you saved her life. Hers and Felix's. You did a good job, Travis."

"I-I gotta find my gear for the snowmobile," I say, dash to the bathroom, and lock the door. The face I see in the mirror is as far from Funeral Face as you can get.

I've saved four cats. Maybe more than four.

Mum would be proud of me. I know she would. The same way Dad was.

After a while, I wash my face. In the front porch, I pull on my helmet so Dad and Dr. Larkin can't see that my eyes are red.

A few minutes later, we all pile onto the snow-mobile, Dr. Larkin behind, me in front squashed against the windshield, the cat trap tied on back. At the top of the last hill, it's as though I see Gulley Cove for the first time. The end shacks look ready to fall into the sea. Waves are leaping at the wharf like a pack of hungry dogs.

When we get off the Ski-Doo at the bottom of the hill, Dr. Larkin looks around. "If we set up the trap, you'd have to check it every day, Travis. It'd be risky leaving a cat in it for too long, because of the cold."

"On the days Travis has hockey, I'll come out on the snowmobile," Dad says. "What are there, four other cats?"

I list them. "Ghost, Rocky, Patches, and Cloud."

We put the trap inside the first shack with cat food for bait, then go home. Dr. Larkin stays for supper—leftover spaghetti and cottage pudding with raisins and caramel sauce. She and Dad are talking away like old friends, and he's calling her Kelsey.

After supper, I spend some time with Felix and actually manage to touch him on his good shoulder without him scratching me. Then I go see Blackie, picking each kitten up and stroking it the way Dr. Larkin showed me. It socializes them, she said, so they won't grow up wild.

Once she's gone home, I call Grady to tell him about the cats now it's not a secret anymore. It takes a long time because he asks so many questions. He thinks it's awesome what I did.

Way cool.

Twenty-seven

Day 322...Knots

We get more snow that night, so I hike over to Abe's after breakfast and bang on the door. "I hurt my wrist, so I can't shovel for a week, Abe. I'm sorry."

He squints at me. "That Quinn feller been after you again?"

"Maybe."

"He's one mean cuss...you oughta tell your dad about him."

"Dad can't follow me around all day. Why don't you show me the barn, so next week I'll know where to shovel?"

We take the path back of the house. Then Abe pushes open a weathered gray door and we go inside the barn. Chickens are pecking in the dirt in a big pen. A pig, three sheep, and the brown and white cow are in stalls at the far end. The barn smells of hay and warm animals. It's clean and the animals are like Lucy—well fed and contented-looking.

"Abe," I say, "why don't you like cats?"

"What's it to ya?"

"You're good to all your animals. But the first day I talked to you, you didn't seem to care that the cats were starving."

"Long story. Not up to jawing about myself much."

"I've got time."

He's rubbing his knuckles up and down the cow's nose. She stands still, her eyes half-closed. "Grew up dirt poor," he says, "and that's the truth. Didn't have a pot to piss in. I was 'bout your age when I found a stray cat in the woods—you sure you want to hear this?"

"Yeah."

"I kept her hidden. Sneaked table scraps to feed her. Then didn't she go and have kittens, three of them. Cute as bugs they were." He clears his throat. "Upshot is m'dad found out and drowned them all in a bucket. So I never as much as looked at a cat since that day."

"Oh, Abe…"

"Don't you go feeling sorry for me…it's a long time ago. Look at me now, an ole geezer. But I shouldn't have spoke so nasty to you that day."

When I try to imagine Dad drowning Blackie and her kittens, I can't get my head around it. But then we've never been dirt poor. At our house, even Felix and Blackie have pots to piss in.

"I needs me mug-up," Abe says, giving the cow one last rub. "Let's go in the house."

His kitchen's big enough for a couch, a table, two chairs, and a potbellied stove that's belching out the heat. All over the walls he's built shelves that hold ships in bottles and model schooners with white sails, their rigging made of string. Hours and hours of work.

Back in the summer when I had Grady to play with, I'd have thought, *Get a life*. Not anymore. Abe takes down a couple of the schooners, letting me hold them while he pours a mug of tea dark as swamp water from the metal pot on the stove. Then he shows me how to tie a bowline and a half hitch. In return, I blow into the whistle Grady gave me and tell Abe how Hud and Marty thought it was a ghost.

I look at my watch and jump up. "Time to go to Gulley Cove; we set a live trap for the cats and I have to check it. That was fun, Abe."

"We'll do a trucker's hitch next time. Watch yourself on that wharf, buddy. And I'll keep me eyes skinned for Hud Quinn."

At the cove, the trap's empty. I lay a trail of food from the hole Hector made in the wall over to the trap, fill the other bowls, and hike home.

I thought for sure there'd be a cat in there today.

Twenty-eight

Day 321...The Numbers' Game

At recess on Monday, I'm talking to Cole and Stevie when I see Hud coming toward us. All too easy to shiver and shake like Blackie, or run for cover like Ghost. But what about Felix, crouched and hissing, claws at the ready?

Hud says, "Can't play hockey because your wrist is sore? Don't see me with no sore wrist."

"What about your gut where I stuck you with the snowshoe? Is that sore?"

Cole's eyes widen and Stevie gives a little gasp. Hud flashes a look around, then turns back to me. "Listen up, wimp—Coach don't like players he can't count on."

"Maybe I'll tell him how I hurt my wrist."

"Squealer, huh?"

"How many goals you score this season, Hud?"

I'm watching his eyes, so when he lashes out with

his fist, I'm ready and I duck. His knuckles slam into the chain-link fence. Another gasp runs around the kids who are watching.

Mrs. Dooks is on yard duty. She usually turns a blind eye on Hud at recess; I should've thought of that before I began mouthing off. Hud grabs me by the shoulder. My boot connects with his shin, but then he bashes my sore wrist against the fence. Pain smothers me in a thick, red fog.

Behind us, a girl starts yelling, "Hud picks on the grade six kids! Hud picks on the grade six kids!"

Hud drops my shoulder. By now, Hector's yelling along with Prinny, loud enough for the whole school to hear. Hector *yelling?* My jaw drops.

"Can it," Hud says in an ugly voice.

But they just shout louder until Cole, Buck, and Stevie join in, their voices thin at first, then getting stronger and stronger, as if they're discovering something new and exciting.

"Shut up!" Hud hollers, and for a moment the voices waver.

Like she's not afraid of anyone, Prinny shouts, "Hud's a bi-ig bul-ly!"

Hector and Cole get in the act, and next thing you know, the schoolyard's rocking. Hud sticks his hands in the pockets of his jacket, turns around, and walks away.

The back of his neck's as red as our hockey jerseys.

When Mrs. Dooks comes on the run, everyone quiets down. But they're all grinning like it's the last day of school.

Specially Prinny and Hector.

Twenty-nine

Days 321 to 312...Stirring the Pot

After school, I hurry over to Prinny's house. If Prinny can stand up to Hud, I can face her dad.

He opens the door.

"Prinny's invited to my house for supper tomorrow night," I say. "She could come over right after school, and she'll be back in time to do her homework."

"She's got supper to cook here," he says and starts to close the door.

I stick my foot in the gap. "Baldwin's has frozen pizza."

"You're some blatherskite!"

"Prinny works hard; it'd be good for her to get out." An idea clicks into my brain. "And Rayleen'll teach her how to cook different stuff. Aren't you tired of canned beans?"

"Maybe Prinny don't want to eat at your place."

"I do want to, Da."

As he turns, I push the door wider. He says to Prinny, "Don't you plan on running the roads every day of the week like your ma."

She tugs at her ponytail. "It's the first time I ever been invited out for supper."

"Okay, okay," he says.

I'm so surprised, I take a step backward. The door shuts in my face and I'm left staring at the peeling paint. He agreed. Wow! Now all I have to do is talk him and Hector's mum into taking one kitten each.

Nothing to it.

Oh yeah, and persuade Rayleen to teach Prinny how to cook.

I run home. "Rayleen, can Prinny Murphy come for supper tomorrow night?"

She sniffs. "I ain't changing the menu. Pot roast and apple crisp."

"That'd be great. Do you think you could show Prinny some stuff about cooking, since you're so good at it? She's making supper for her dad now her mother's not there."

"Past time he gave that woman the boot," Rayleen says.

"I don't think her ma ever taught her much about cooking."

"There's not a Quinn born that's good for anything."

"Prinny is!"

"You sweet on her, Travis?"

Heat creeps up my neck. "I bet her dad would be nicer to her if he's fed better."

"No flies on you, boyo. I'll show her how I makes a crisp, how about it? Now you better go check that cat trap."

At Gulley Cove, the trap's empty. Second day in a row.

❧

When Prinny comes over after school on Tuesday, looking like she doesn't know what to do with her hands and feet, Rayleen takes over. She wraps an apron around Prinny and sits her down with the recipe. We all chop the apples, then Prinny mixes oatmeal, brown sugar, and melted butter for the topping.

"Hardest part is reading the recipe," Prinny says. "Can you teach me how to do pastry? Da sure likes his moose-meat pie."

With her clean hair and a big smile on her face, she looks a lot different from the Prinny I first saw on the bus. Rayleen shrugs. "How about you come over here every Tuesday? That's the day they've cut back on the soaps."

Prinny looks like she's been given ten kittens. "That's real nice of you, Rayleen."

Now it's Rayleen's turn to look hot under the collar. "I guess you might as well hang around and watch me baste the meat and taters," she mutters. "Travis, you cut up that cabbage."

And I thought I'd get to watch TV for once.

❧

In the next week, we catch Patches and Ghost. Dr. Larkin keeps them long enough that they recover from surgery, then they go back to Gulley Cove. I don't feel too good about this, but there's no more room in our house, and she says it would take a long time to tame them because they're so wild.

Felix has his stitches out, although he still walks a bit stiff. He lets me pat him now. With the door to the back porch shut tight, we sometimes give him the run of the house. He roams around, howling every now and then, poking his nose into all the corners. Then he settles back in his room.

Hud hasn't come near me since the day the kids yelled at him. I keep hoping he's forgotten about me. How dumb is that. Specially since I'm back to playing hockey and scoring goals.

Hud's just biding his time. Making me squirm.

Hector's been over after school to see the kittens. He wants one, but figures once they start running around with their sharp little claws, they'd make a big mess of his mother's living room.

"You should take Blackie instead," I hear myself say. "She's laid-back. Your mum would like Blackie."

He grunts. But I can tell he's thinking about it.

So am I. I wish I'd never suggested it; I'd much rather Blackie lived with me. But I'm the only one who'd want Felix with his lopped-off ears and his goalie crouch; or Cloud and Patches, who take off if you look at them sideways. So I guess I have to give Blackie away, even though she's special.

As for Prinny, she's already made pot roast. "Da liked it," she says. "The apple crisp, too." Her mother hasn't come home, although Prinny's been over to Fiddlers Cove once to see her.

Then Prinny's name shows up on the December birthday list in our classroom. So I go over to her place on the Tuesday she's at my place making pastry with Rayleen.

I knock on the front door, as edgy as if I'm waiting to go on the ice during playoffs. When Prinny's father opens the door, I gabble, "We got a cute little kitten that needs a home. Can we give it to Prinny for her birthday? Although she can't take it from its mother for another five or six weeks."

He's scowling at me. Like the Crusher. "You're some bucky," he says.

"Prinny'd love to have a kitten. She'd look after it, and she's doing her best to learn new stuff from Rayleen."

"How come Prinny never mentioned no kitten?"

"She's scared you'll say no."

He looks like *no* is right there on the tip of his tongue. He scratches his head, his eyes squinched up. "She's in school all day. Who looks after the kitten then?"

"You could take two! That way they'd keep each other company. The cat had two kittens—one gray and one ginger. Prinny would never expect to get both of them. She'd jump high as the moon."

I'm pushing my luck. But Prinny's dad looks different than he used to. Maybe he feels better now his wife's not around spilling wine and smashing TVs.

He says, "You got m'head mazed. Come back and see me tomorrow."

"You'll keep it a secret though? We gotta surprise her."

"You come back tomorrow," he says and closes the door. Another big flake of paint's coming off by the knob.

∽

On Wednesday, Cloud's in the trap, spitting and snarling. So off he goes to the vet. After supper I walk over to Prinny's house. Her dad steps outside when he sees it's me. "Okay," he says.

My mouth drops open. "You'll take the kittens? Both of them?"

"That's what I'm after telling you."

"Prinny'll be so happy! We're inviting her for supper on her birthday next Tuesday. Why don't you come? Do you like roast chicken and chocolate fudge cake?"

"You ever run out of ideas?"

"I'll ask Rayleen to set a place for you. She's a great cook."

"I got no fit-out for that."

"Wear what you got on."

"Huh," he says, then backs up and closes the door. Quietly, for him.

I run up the street to Hector's. His mother says, "Why, Travis, do come in, dearie. Isn't it desperate cold? I'm sick of the snow already and it's not even Christmas. It's so nice you and Hector are friends. Do you want to see him? He's in the workshop with his father, but I can fetch him."

"It's you I want to see."

The living room's crammed with lace mats, fake roses, and china lighthouses. "Hector and me rescued some cats that were starving," I say, not mentioning where we found them. "One of them's had kittens, then she'll go to the vet to be spayed. She's a very quiet cat. Will you let Hector take her?"

"A *cat?*"

"She'd be no trouble. Her name's Blackie. She doesn't want to be outdoors anymore. My dad says she's had a hard life. He thinks the person who takes her will be doing a good deed."

I'm not really lying. I know Dad would think that way. He's just never said so.

"Oh," she says.

And that's all she says. Sort of a miracle. Except *no* is only one word too, and it's the one I'm worried about. "You could come over to our place and meet Blackie. She's living in the back porch for now; she hasn't done any damage to anything. She's a good mother, and the vet says she's healthy."

I'm sounding desperate, so I shut up. Seems like I've shut Hector's mum up as well. If she won't take Blackie, Hector'll be disappointed, and I don't know who else to ask. Rayleen's already warned me not to put the touch on her.

"Well," Mrs. Baldwin says, "I'd have to see the cat first. Perhaps she could stay downstairs most of the time—Hector's bedroom is down there."

I don't give her time to change her mind. "Dad's home tonight because he doesn't have clinic. Why don't you come over in half an hour?"

I race home and tell Dad he has to do a big sales pitch on Hector's mum because she thinks he's someone pretty special, being a doctor and all. He gives me one of his looks and says he'll do his best.

Sharp at eight, Hector's mum knocks on the door. We give her a cup of tea along with some of Rayleen's butterscotch squares, then she and Dad talk on and on about the weather and the local council. Finally she puts her cup down.

Dad says to her, "Would you like to see the cat?"

We troop to the back porch. The kittens are asleep. Blackie looks up and licks her front paw.

Hector's mum doesn't say anything. I'm scared she'll turn us down flat, now that Blackie's not just an idea but an actual cat with fur and whiskers.

Dad says, "I think it's good for children to have pets, Mrs. Baldwin. It can teach them valuable lessons about responsibility...wouldn't you agree?"

"Oh yes," she says faintly.

"Travis is an only child, and now that your older sons have left home, Hector's in effect an only child as well. Helpful for him to have the company of a pet."

"I hadn't thought of it that way."

"We will, of course, look after spaying the cat."

"That's very kind."

You gotta admire Dad: Hector's mum looks like she's been hypnotized. She leans over, holding out one hand as if she's afraid Blackie might munch on it for supper. "Hello, Blackie."

Blackie yawns.

"She seems very calm," Hector's mum says. "How long before Hector could have her?"

"Six or seven weeks," Dad says.

"That would give me plenty of time to prepare…It might be nice to have a cat in the house…it gets lonesome sometimes when Hector and his dad are in the workshop."

"Then everyone's happy," Dad says.

After she leaves, he gives me a high-five and we each have another butterscotch square.

Thirty

Day 311...Twisted

So everything's going fine the next afternoon when I snowshoe the shortcut to Gulley Cove. I'm later than usual because Rayleen wanted me to run to the store for her.

I'm filling the bowls in the fourth shack, being quiet because I caught a glimpse of Rocky hanging around outside, when I hear the faraway grumble of a snowmobile engine. Dad must have gotten off work early, and he's brought Cloud back from the vet. That's neat. Means I don't have to hike home.

Rocky slithers through the gap in the boards. He goes "*Aaaiiiooowww*" when he sees me, his lips pulled back to show his teeth. The snowmobile's louder now, and his ears twitch uneasily. But as the engine cuts out, he buries his nose in the food bowl.

I don't want Dad to leave without me, so I edge toward the opening. Rocky lets out another long wail, then streaks through the gap. But at least he didn't run right away.

I walk along the edge of the wharf, listening to the waves *whump* against the rocks. Dad must be inside the first shack checking the trap, because the door's open. The stick I used the night the dogs were here is still propped against the wall. I creep closer, planning to spook him by yowling like Ghost.

A loud thud inside the shack nearly makes me fall off the wharf. Another thud, the sharp crack of wood splintering, then the snap of split plastic and rattle of cat food spilling on the floor.

I stop dead, icy with fear. Hud.

Run for the trees. Blow my whistle. Call Dad on the cell phone. Call 911.

Hud could follow my tracks in the snow and I doubt he believes in ghosts anymore. I'm fumbling for the phone when I hear him grunt louder than Hector. Metal scrapes metal, setting my teeth on edge. A cat gives a piercing cry, so close the hair bristles on the back of my neck.

I didn't check the trap when I got here. Not even Hud would smash a trap with a cat inside... would he?

My boots feel like they're frozen to the wharf.

On the other side of the wall, Hud laughs. "Can't get away, can ya?" The trap thumps against the shack wall; the cat screeches.

Rage erases every rule Dad ever made. I seize the stick and rush into the shack. Ghost's in the trap, which is bent way out of shape. His mouth's stretched wide and he's shuddering.

Hud's poised to kick the trap again. His head whips around. I slam the stick down on his shoulder like I'm sixteen years old and seven feet tall. He howls in pain, staggering sideways.

"I hate you!" I scream. "I hate your guts!"

I ram the stick into his chest. He braces himself against the wall and surges toward me, murder in his eyes.

I back away, fast. He laughs. "Once I'm done with you, I'm gonna drown the cat—throw it in the sea, trap and all."

He takes a run at me. I step backward to the edge of the wharf, heartbeat on fast-forward, every detail sharp and clear. At the very last second, I thrust the stick out.

Hud trips over it and jackknifes off the wharf. In a fountain of spray and a swirl of ripples, he's swallowed by the sea.

That's when I notice his helmet lying near the door. I loop my hand in the strap; as he rears up, water streaming off his snowmobile suit, I aim for the far end of the wharf and throw the helmet into the sea. Then I dart into the shack, pick up the trap, and race for the shortcut.

My snowshoes are stuck toe-up in a drift. Fingers shaking, I stretch the bindings over my boots, grab the trap again, and lunge up the hill. *Hud don't like to walk*...that's what Prinny said.

I threw his helmet into shallow water so he'd be sure to go after it, giving me time to get away. All I have to do is reach Abe's.

What if he drowns?

My steps falter. The undertow nearly got me when I was wearing jeans. Hud's in a snowmobile suit and boots.

He's a lot taller and stronger than me.

I charge up the next slope, the trap banging against my leg. Ghost's heavy and my wrist, the one Hud sprained, has been hurting ever since I bashed him with the stick.

Because the shortcut's a tumble of rocks and boulders, he can't follow me on the snowmobile. I'm way more skillful on snowshoes now; I pick my way through the rocks, stepping on deeper snow whenever I can. In the first grove of trees, I take a moment to look back.

I don't hate Hud so bad that I want him to drown.

He comes around the corner of the end shack,

carrying his helmet, dragging his feet. I duck behind the trees, relief and terror jacking my heart rate up another notch.

Move, Travis. Move. Not sparing the breath to talk to Ghost, who's hunkered down in the bottom of the trap, his eyes like black pits, I swing the snowshoes as fast as I can without tripping over the rocks. A couple of minutes later, I reach the crest of the hill.

Far below, the snowmobile snarls to life.

My brain knows I'm safe on the shortcut. The rest of me doesn't. *Faster, faster…*When Felix was hurt, I ran all the way to Abe's. I can do it again.

By now, the shortcut's angled away from the track. But the wind's onshore, and the snowmobile sounds all too close. Then, gradually, the sound recedes.

Hud's ahead of me. He's cold and he's wet, and I'm hoping he'll head straight to Fiddlers Cove. I also hope the whole freaking community sees him looking like a drowned rat.

A drowned cat…

"Ghost," I gasp, "you're gonna be okay. I won't let Hud near you ever again."

The trees are thinning out, their trunks black in the dusk. Against the sky, a thin column of smoke rises from Abe's chimney. I head toward it, eyes searching the shadows, ears straining for the sound of the snowmobile.

Hud could be hidden among the spruce trees, waiting for me. I suddenly realize he must have known about me helping the cats when he went to Gulley Cove today, because there's no other reason for him to be there. Likely Rayleen made Felix's rescue into a big drama, and it wouldn't have taken long for the word to spread.

He'd smashed Blackie's shelter to pieces, the edges of the wood raw and sharp, bits of Styrofoam skittering over the floorboards like snowflakes. He's no different than people on the news channel who blow up school buses just to show they can.

Easy enough to pay for a new trap and replace the cat dish.

But it isn't just things that get broken.

I circle behind Abe's place, using trees and boulders for cover. Lucy's in the yard and barks at me. Ghost gives a low yowl. I move out into the open, lift the trap as high as I can, and head for the front door.

"Down, Lucy. Down!"

Then Abe comes around the house in his rubber boots and overalls. My body sags, breath rasping in my ears, arms trembling. I've never been so glad to see anyone in my life.

I'm safe from Hud. And so's Ghost.

"Time for barn chores," Abe says. "What you got there?"

184

The barn...I stare at him, my jaw dropping. But I'm not seeing him. I'm seeing the pig rooting in the vegetable peelings, the cow chewing her cud...the barn warm, smelling of hay.

"That's the perfect place!"

"You lost me, b'y."

"The barn—it's perfect."

Lucy's dancing around me. Ghost hisses. "Down, Lucy!" Abe says, and Lucy sits down. "What's up with the cat?"

"His name's Ghost. I need a place for him. A safe place. Hud was at the cove. He smashed Blackie's shelter."

"That's right spitey."

"Cloud, the little gray cat, is at the vet's. But two other cats are still at the cove. Hud could go back anytime on his snowmobile. Abe, if I trap the two cats and bring them here, can they stay in the barn along with Ghost and Cloud? I'd feed them every day and try taming them so we could find proper homes for them." My face falls. "But there's Lucy. Dogs chase cats, don't they?"

"Only thing she chases is hornets—got the brains of a turnip, that dog."

"If the cats were in the barn, I wouldn't have to worry about Hud, or dogs killing them. Or blizzards. Besides, they'd keep the mice down."

"First sensible thing you've said." Abe fishes in his pocket, pulls out a Kit Kat bar like it's the winning Lotto ticket, and passes it to me. "I had a sister like you. She'd get this idea and run with it, and first thing you know I'd be running right alongside her. She got me in more trouble than there's capelin in July-month."

He's saying no.

I can't take Ghost back to Gulley Cove. In desperation, even though it'll remind Abe of his dad, I say, "Hud was going to drown Ghost. Throw him into the sea in the trap."

Abe stares at me. His eyes are a faded blue, like jeans you've washed a lot.

"How'd you stop him?"

"Tripped him so he fell off the wharf."

Abe snorts with laughter. "Not much stumps you, my son."

"Please, Abe—I don't know what else to do!"

He scratches his head. "Don't reckon cats would bother the pigs or the sheep none. The hens is in a separate pen; cats couldn't touch them there. Lots of hay in the loft and I milks the cow twice a day, no reason the cats couldn't have a few squirts. Eat that bar, buddy."

I peel back the wrapper, wishing he'd hurry up.

"I been bothered some with mice getting in the

feed," he says. "Wouldn't do no harm to have a cat or two around."

"Two cats? Or four?"

"You gotta catch 'em first."

"We could bait the trap with canned tuna."

He sticks out his hand. "It's a deal. Tell you what, them cats got lucky the day you went to Gulley Cove."

"Thanks, Abe," I quaver, so relieved I'm close to bawling like a baby. "Thanks a million."

He pats me on the back like I'm Lucy. "Get on with you. Although I gotta tell you—if a cat made up its mind, it could find a way outta that barn quicker'n a pig'll fart."

Leave a warm, dry barn for snow and rocks and a pack of dogs? No cat would be that crazy. "Can we take Ghost there now? There's cat food in my pack."

"I'll find a dish or two in the kitchen."

Abe brings three bowls from the house, and we set Ghost up in a corner at the back of the barn with food, water, and his own pile of hay. Abe tugs on the cow's udder and puts a bowl of milk near the trap. Then he levers the door open.

Ghost crouches as far back in the trap as he can. He's shivering.

"The barn's the best place for you," I whisper. "Don't run away into the woods, Ghost. Stay here where it's safe."

"Once he's outta there, I can fix the trap," Abe says. "Bang it back into shape."

"You can? That'd be great—I didn't know how I was going to tell Dr. Larkin. And Dad would go ballistic if he knew what happened."

"Nothing to it. Now, I'll drive you home in case that Quinn feller's lying in wait at the bend in the road."

That's not an offer I'm about to refuse. Today I saw a side of Hud I never saw before. Feral doesn't cover it; he was way beyond feral. Manic, berserk, totally out of control...as though he had to wreck something or go crazy.

I don't want to see that side of him again. Ever.

Underneath all this, another thought's lurking. I lost control, too. When I smashed the stick down on his shoulder, it wasn't just to stop him; I did it to hurt.

Mum wouldn't be too happy about that.

When I get home, Rayleen's in the kitchen stirring the stew, the radio tuned to the tag end of the news. I wait for her to blast me for being late.

"Who needs the news in St. John's?" she says, turning the radio off. "Big news in Fiddlers Cove. Someone set fire to the old chandler's store, and it's burning clear to the ground. Lucky thing it was empty. Volunteer fire departments come from as far as St. Christopher and Blandings, but they can't do much except watch.

Arson, they say—the cops got a suspect already. I'd bet any money it's a Quinn, the whole crew of them ain't worth pork scraps."

If someone told me from the day I was born that the Keatings were good for nothing, how would I have turned out?

Thirty-one

Day 310...Alibi

First thing Friday morning, Dad and me pick up Cloud at the vet's. Although the bill's adding up, Dad's cool with it so far; he said we'd have a talk later on about all the expenses and figure out how much I should be contributing out of my allowance. When I tell Dr. Larkin about Abe's barn, she thinks it's a brilliant solution.

Then we take Cloud to Abe's place. Turns out Dad used to make ships in bottles when he was a kid, so he and Abe hit it off right away. Cloud goes into the barn, and we drive home in a big rush so I can get ready for school.

Hud doesn't get on the bus that morning. But the other kids from Fiddlers Cove are talking up a storm. Hud's been charged with arson. Someone reported him lurking around the chandler's store five minutes before it went up in flames.

"What time did they see him?" I ask Cole, trying to sound casual.

"Round about four-thirty, they said."

At twenty after four, Hud was smashing Blackie's shelter in Gulley Cove. "Who reported him?"

"Old Danny Grimsby. Used to be the best dory man in the cove. His brain's a bit addled, but he swears up and down it was Hud. Not that the Grimsbys ever had much truck with the Quinns."

Another Fiddlers Cove kid chimes in. "The cops kept Hud for questioning. He could go to juvie for this." He snickers. "None of us'll miss him."

No Hud to grind my face into the road or destroy everything I've worked for at Gulley Cove? Anyone who'd miss him has granite for brains.

If I keep quiet, a whole lot of kids will be a whole lot happier. Including me.

But Hud didn't burn the store down.

❧

On the way home on the bus, Prinny tells me Hud's her first cousin; his father and her mother are brother and sister. "Hud's da has a short fuse—quick with his fists, Ma always said. As for Hud's ma, when God was handing out backbones, He skipped her altogether."

I'm not going to feel sorry for Hud Quinn. I am not.

Dad gets home early so he can drive me to hockey at five; I wear the wrist brace he gave me. At the arena, everyone's talking about the fire. Hud hasn't been arrested, but the cops aren't done with him.

If he's all caught up talking to the police, he won't be heading for the cove this weekend. I'll reset the trap tomorrow. I just hope Patches and Rocky will go for the bait, so I can take them to the barn. Company for Ghost and Cloud, assuming they're still there.

When we get home from hockey, Dad tosses the local paper on the end of the table. We race out to Gulley Cove on the snowmobile after supper, but the trap's empty. Before I go to bed, I sneak the newspaper into my room. The article includes photos of the fire, the fire trucks, Danny Grimsby, and the local police corporal; it gives the exact time the suspect was allegedly seen but doesn't give his name because he's underage. The article ends by saying, *If anyone witnessed anything of a suspicious nature in the vicinity of the chandler's store in Fiddlers Cove, would they notify the RCMP Detachment in St. Fabien immediately.*

That lets me off the hook. I wasn't anywhere near the store.

Thirty-two

Days 309 and 308...Lying, Levels 1 and 2

At the rink on Saturday, the guys all talk to me in the dressing room; as usual, being on the ice makes me feel tall as Dad. But as the day goes by, I start shrinking. I don't want Hector or Prinny going with me to Gulley Cove and seeing the damage Hud did the day of the fire, so I have to fudge my way through that without actually lying. Hector just grunts, but Prinny looks hurt.

Abe's straightened the trap nearly as good as new. As usual, he goes fidgety when I thank him. "Cat food and milk were gone this morning," he says, "but I didn't lay eyes on the cats. Skedaddled to the loft when they heard me, likely."

At the cove, I bait the trap with special cat treats I bought at Baldwin's. Then I throw the Styrofoam and pieces of wood in a garbage bag. If Hud's dad is quick with fists, like Abe's dad was, why did Abe turn out decent and Hud meaner than a cornered weasel?

Kicking a cat and threatening to drown it. Anger bubbles up in me again.

Later on, Dad and I snowmobile to the barrens on the groomed trails, and end up having Chinese food in St. Fabien. But I can't shake that shrinking feeling.

Keeping quiet about the truth's pretty much the same as telling a lie, and lies tangle you up worse than a mess of fish rope. If I get Hud off the hook, though, the guys at school will think I'm a total loser. Plus Hud'll still be around, throwing the little kids' lunch cans in the snow, boasting about the crows he's shot with his .22, ambushing me any chance he gets.

Rule #2: No Lying.

Dad acted like it was okay I'd lied to save the cats. So now I'm lying to save kids and crows.

Same difference.

❧

I wake up early on Sunday with a pain in my stomach. Dad sleeps in. At breakfast, as he smears jelly on his toast, he says, "Do you know the boy accused of setting the fire in Fiddlers Cove?"

My spoon splats into my cereal. Milk sprays the placemat. "Uh…no. Well, sort of."

"Clean up the mess," Dad says. "What's his name?"

194

"He's not in my grade." I push back from the table and head for the sink. "Hud Quinn."

"A Quinn from Fiddlers Cove—that's a strike against him from the start. Is he a decent guy?"

I'm busy wringing water from the cloth. "He's okay."

"He's not the one who hurt your wrist, is he?"

I shake my head; that way, I'm not actually speaking a lie.

"Do you know anything about this fire, Travis?"

Even though Dad can't match Prinny's father when it comes to suspicious, he's still no slouch.

"I was at Gulley Cove when the fire was set," I say. "We've got an extra hockey practice today, because the gentlemen's league was canceled and Coach says we need the ice time. Can you take me to the rink for eleven-thirty?"

"We'll get your skates sharpened while we're there."

So the subject of Hud is dropped.

Before the game, when we're in the dressing room taping our pads and lacing our skates, Stevie says, "I heard Hud's locked in the basement of his house."

"The shed," Buck says. "His dad locked him in the shed." He gives a mock shiver. "Chained to the wall."

"Being tortured," Allan Corkum says. He's got curly hair and baby-blue eyes, and Hud picks on him a lot.

"Council won't let Hud's dad have dogs anymore," Cole says. "He used to beat on them."

"Pretty soon he won't have Hud, either," Stevie says.

"Neither'll we," Allan says, jamming his helmet over his curls and grinning through his mouth guard.

Hud's not chained in the shed any more than Joe Baldwin saw a ghost at Gulley Cove with slime dripping off its skull.

But maybe the police threw him in a cell.

I don't say this. I don't want to talk about it.

We have a short warm-up, then divide into two teams—Reds and Blues—and have a game. I miss a drop pass, fan on a shot, then shoot the puck right at the goalie's chest pad. Another shot hits the post, then I trip over someone's skate and land, *whap,* on my hip. I score exactly one goal, and that was more or less a fluke.

Afterward, no one says anything, but they don't need to. I'm doing a big enough number on myself. Too bad I can't use my sore wrist as an excuse...*oh, I hurt it hitting Hud at Gulley Cove at the same time he was setting the fire at the chandler's store.*

After hockey, Dad takes me to the cove on the Ski-Doo to check the trap. It's empty again. The stick's lying on the wharf, and a fleck of Styrofoam's caught in the boards.

Any way I turn, I'm thinking about Hud. I wonder who *did* set the fire. They must be having a good laugh.

Thirty-three

Day 307...Witness

My alarm goes off early on Monday, and I snowshoe to the cove before the sun's properly up. I woke up with the same shrinking feeling I had all day yesterday. The barrens don't help—they always make me feel small.

Arguments are zapping back and forth in my head like two players passing the puck.

After I told Prinny to wash her hair, I felt guilty, yeah. Chickadee-sized guilt. This guilt's more like a bull moose in full charge. If Hud gets sent to juvie, he may never come back. It'll take him away from his parents and his home. It'll change his whole life.

And I'll be the one responsible.

No one will know it's my fault.

Hud'll know. And he's the type to remember. I'll always be looking back over my shoulder, no matter how old I am.

When push comes to shove, maybe he'll blab about being in Gulley Cove, and then it'll all come out, including the fact I kept my mouth shut when I shouldn't have. Jeez, will I get grounded for that. I won't be allowed near a rink until I'm thirty-five.

But if I go to the cops, Cole, Buck, and Stevie'll never speak to me again; that's what I'm really afraid of. Back to square one, recess standing alone by the fence.

If I shrink any smaller, I'll disappear.

It's a relief to arrive at the cove, even more of a relief to find Rocky in the trap. The look on his face reminds me of Mrs. Dooks.

Every time Mrs. Dooks turns her back on Hud in the schoolyard, she's as much as lying. Do I want to be like her?

"Rocky," I say, "why don't you tell me what to do?" Rocky spits at me. The one question I've been avoiding is what Mum would say, and that's because I know the answer. Mum would have driven me to the police detachment the day of the fire.

When I call Dad on the cell phone, he says he can take Rocky to the vet on his way to work. He comes out to Gulley Cove on the Ski-Doo, we load Rocky on, and head home. Next, I phone Abe.

"Cats are still in the barn," Abe says. "Won't let me near 'em, though."

"We caught another one this morning. His name's Rocky. Dad's taking him to the vet."

"Them mice better pack their bags."

On the school bus, I huddle into my seat. When Hud gets on, he walks past as though the back of the bus is the only thing worth looking at. He's wearing shades, his collar pulled up. As his jacket brushes against my seat, I feel the vibes clear down to my toes. *Visceral* is another word I misspelled in English class. Who'd have thought it had a *c* in it?

No way I'm going anywhere near a police station for Hud Quinn. Let him hang.

School goes by in a blur. I've got a pain in my stomach again even though the guys are talking to me, and even though Prinny manages to read a whole paragraph out loud with only three mistakes. On the trip home, she and Hector sit in their usual seats on the other side of the bus, looking out the window, not talking to each other or to me. Neither one of them's been over-friendly since the weekend.

Hud's the last one off in Fiddlers Cove. Although it's cloudy now, he's still wearing his shades. They're big, like aviator glasses. I watch him out my window. He doesn't look as tall walking toward his house as he does in the schoolyard.

As Mr. Murphy pulls the lever on the door and puts the bus in gear, the engine roaring like a bulldozer, a man comes around the side of the house, wearing an old red-checked hunting jacket and rubber boots. He's bigger than Hud, with a stubble of beard on his chin. He walks right up to Hud, as if he's going to help him with his school books, and smashes him in the mouth with his fist so hard that Hud's thrown against the shed.

I make this sound in my throat and leap to my feet. Blood trickles down Hud's chin, his shades are crooked, and he's braced for another blow. As the bus lurches away from the stop, I fall backward into my seat.

Over my shoulder, I see the man's lips move as he says something to Hud. Then he marches into the house and slams the door behind him.

Dazed, I look around. Prinny and Hector didn't even notice. Mr. Murphy's busy watching the road, humming away to himself, so I know he didn't see anything.

When Hud got me against the locker, there was a yellowing bruise on his neck.

I've watched wrestling on TV, although not when Dad's around. And once on the sports channel, I saw part of a boxing match—two guys punching each other so hard that sweat sprayed the air. But in real life I never saw a father drive his fist into his kid's face. Deliberately, the only aim to hurt.

When Hector and Prinny get off the bus, I don't say anything. At my stop, I walk right past Mr. Murphy, mumbling good-bye on my way down the steps. Mira and Flint are having a major fight on TV, so Rayleen doesn't notice anything's wrong. I go straight to the back porch, sit down, and hold the kittens close to my chest.

As if somehow I can protect them from everything that's going on outside our door.

Thirty-four

Day 307...The Truth, the Whole Truth

Rayleen leaves as soon as Dad walks in. The smell of baked cod turning my stomach, I say, "I gotta talk to the police in St. Fabien, Dad. Right away. It's about the fire in Fiddlers Cove."

Dad has this look that's like an X-ray, seeing right through you. He doesn't use it often, but he's using it now. "What's up?"

"I need to talk to a policeman, that's all."

"I wondered if you knew something about the fire." He checks the number and picks up the phone. When he puts it down, he says, "There's someone still at the detachment; he'll wait for us. Brush your hair and put on a clean shirt."

So it's too late to change my mind. The stone in my gut is as big as a boulder. We drive to St. Fabien, me wishing we'd never arrive, and pull up by a brick building that has a sign out front with a fancy crest. *Maintiens le Droit*, it says. Maintain the Right.

It's not that simple.

We ring the bell. The policeman's wearing a beige shirt and navy pants with a wide yellow stripe down each leg. He smiles at us. "Corporal Deakins," he says.

Dad introduces us and we sit down in the office. I say, talking fast, "I saw Hud Quinn in Gulley Cove on the day of the fire. He came on a snowmobile. He was there from about four-fifteen to quarter to five. So he couldn't have set the fire."

The policeman's got the X-ray stare down pat, too. He pulls a pad toward him and picks up a pen. "You're sure about the time?"

"I always wear my watch so I'll get home before dark."

"What was Hud doing at the cove?"

"He was busting some stuff—a wooden cat shelter and an animal trap. I've been feeding a bunch of cats out there."

"He smashed the trap?" Dad says. "Why?"

He and the corporal are both staring at me.

"Hud doesn't like me; never has. I'm a townie and I score too many goals at hockey. He found out I was looking after the cats, and I guess it was a way for him to get even."

Before the corporal can open his mouth, Dad says, "So it *was* Hud who sprained your wrist."

I kick the table leg. "Yeah."

"Is that why you didn't tell me about the fire right away?"

"Guess so."

The corporal takes over. "We've got Hud pegged as the school bully. We'll be going to the principal and addressing that issue separately. Travis, are you prepared to sign an official statement about what you've just told me?"

I nod. The corporal turns his seat to the computer, pulls up a form, and asks us a bunch of questions, typing in the answers. He prints the form, lets me and Dad read it, then I sign it with Dad as witness. The corporal stands up. "We really appreciate your help with our investigation, Travis. Thanks, Dr. Keating."

We walk outside, past the sign, and get in the Toyota. There's two pictures in my head. Hud's dad driving his fist into his son's face. And me at recess when the guys find out I got Hud off the hook. They'll find out—I'd bet my new graphite hockey stick on it. If Stevie, Cole, and Buck go back to the silent treatment, I'm finished.

We go in the house. I've been wearing the brace again because my wrist is still sore; the slap shots I took yesterday didn't help. I feel like ripping the brace off and throwing it at the wall. Or at Hud. Or Dad.

I feel like breaking every rule in the book.

"Sit down, Travis," Dad says.

"I don't want to."

"I have to know if Hud's been bullying you ever since we moved here."

"So you can fix it? Oh sure. You're good at that."

The X-ray look is back full force. *Tick, tick, tick* goes the clock. "What do you mean?" Dad says.

"Nothing."

"Come on, Travis. I need to know about Hud. Did he threaten you, so you were scared to tell me?"

"What's the use of telling *you*?" There goes Rule #5: Mind Your Manners.

"I could have intervened."

"You can't fix everything! You didn't fix Mum."

There's five seconds of dead silence. "We're not talking about your mother," Dad says sharply. "We're talking about Hud."

"Right. You never talk about Mum, you're scared to because you didn't make her better. When I was little, she told me that's what a doctor's job was all about."

This time the silence seems to last forever. "So for the last year you've been *blaming* me for your mother's death?"

"I never thought she'd die!"

"But I told you how sick she was," Dad says. "I warned you."

"I didn't believe you. I was sure you'd find a way to save her."

"I couldn't," Dad says. And that's all he says. He looks like every rock in Gulley Cove is piled on his shoulders.

I glare at him as if he'd murdered her. "You went to medical school to learn how to fix people. So why didn't you just *do* it?"

He leans forward. "I fought for your mother's life as hard as I could...and she fought just as hard. But the cancer won in the end. It wasn't anyone's fault!"

"At the funeral, I kept waiting for her to walk in the church and say it was all a mistake."

"You never told me that before," Dad says.

Now he looks like the rocks are crushing him. I'm still angry, even though I know I shouldn't be. "You never talk about her anymore."

"You told me not to—yelled at me, remember?"

"You've forgotten all about her."

"Travis, I'll never forget her," he says, painfully slow. "She was a huge part of my life. Watching her die, feeling so damned helpless...it was the hardest thing I've ever done."

Funny thing is, I believe him right away, and the anger's gone. *Phhht.* Just like that. He clears his throat.

"Besides, she gave me you. You'll always be her son just as much as mine."

I take a deep breath past the tightness in my own throat. "Maybe we could start talking about her again…now and then."

"I'd like that. Very much."

"I still miss her," I say in a thick voice that doesn't sound like mine.

"Yes," Dad says. Just one word, but I know he gets it. Then he grabs hold of me like he'll drown if he doesn't.

"I've been mad at you ever since she died," I say into the buttons on his shirt. "Moving here made it worse, because she felt so far away."

"She's always close, no matter where you are."

"It was like I'd lost both of you."

I never thought I'd tell him that. He holds onto me so tight I can hardly breathe. "Love you," he says.

"You too," I mumble.

Seems like Hud did us a good turn.

Thirty-five

Day 306...Recount: Day 1

By 8 a.m. on Tuesday, Dad and me have picked up Rocky at the vet's and driven him to Abe's barn. I catch sight of a white tail whipping into a stall, so I know Ghost's around. Rocky sneaks out of the trap before we even leave the barn, his whiskers and nose quivering. I bet he's smelling the other cats; maybe that'll encourage him to stay put.

When Prinny gets on the school bus, her ponytail's as shiny as can be, with a new green ribbon around it that matches her green sweater. I hope her dad gave them to her.

"Happy birthday," I say.

She tilts her nose in the air. "Thank you," she says, deadly polite.

"Prinny, the reason I didn't want you going to the cove on the weekend is because Hud bust the shelter the day of the fire, and I wasn't going to tell anyone. But yesterday I told the police so he wouldn't go to reform school."

Her eyes widen. "Aunt Ida said it was some fire. She thinks Sam Herbey set it; he's been playing with matches since he was four, and he's sixteen now." Her eyes go even wider. "You spoke up for Hud after all he did to you? That was real nice of you."

"Nice? Or nutso?"

"In church we learned you're supposed to do good to them that spitefully use you." She shrugs. "I tried it with two of the girls at school—can't say it got me anywheres."

The bus stops to pick up Hector. Mr. Murphy says, smiling at me over his shoulder, "Even a guy as mean as Hud shouldn't get in trouble for something he didn't do. You did the right thing, Travis...don't let anyone tell you different."

Hector climbs up the steps and sits down. After I go through it all again, he grunts—a grunt I can't decipher.

"You think I'm out in left field?"

"My dad says you gotta follow the grain of the wood. Isn't that what you did?"

"Guess so."

End of discussion. We drive to Fiddlers Cove talking about this and that, and stop outside Hud's house. He gets on the bus. There's a cut at the corner of his mouth and his jaw's swollen; another cut sits right over his eye. I suppose that's why he was wearing shades yesterday.

He stops in the aisle and looks right at me. "You went to the cops. You weird me out, man."

"You're welcome," I say, and for a split second Hud's smile—I swear—is the nearest thing to a real smile. Then he scowls and kicks at the seat as if he's got to kick something.

"I never come across the likes of you before," he says, and plods down the aisle.

It's neat he hasn't figured me out. But him standing that close to me, even for a minute or two, made my skin crawl. I don't think he'll quit being a bully just because I cleared him with the cops. That'd be like expecting Felix to rub his head against my knee the first time I fed him.

❧

At recess, the guys on the hockey team crowd around me, wanting to know how I got Hud off the arson charge.

"When he was supposed to be setting the fire, he was at Gulley Cove," I say. "I saw him there."

"Better for all of us if he'd gone to juvie," Buck says.

Stevie shrugs. "Isn't it better for the cops to catch the guy who *did* set the fire? Next time he might burn someone's house down."

Cole and Buck both live in Fiddlers Cove. "I bet it

was Sam Herbey," Cole says. "I don't want him setting fire to our place."

"But we're still stuck with Hud," Buck says.

"We could try hanging out in groups," Stevie says. "Remember how he backed off when everyone yelled?"

"Yeah—that was awesome," Cole says. "Come on, let's play ball hockey. We only got ten minutes left."

"Got your stick, Travis?" Buck says.

So the guys are still talking to me. Huge relief.

I play like I'm Sidney Crosby and Alexander Ovechkin rolled into one.

❧

Once Hector's off the bus that afternoon, I say to Prinny, "After your cooking lesson with Rayleen, you can play with the kittens. Their eyes are open and they're starting to stagger around."

"Then I gotta go home to cook supper," she says.

She takes off her coat in the porch and says hi to Rayleen. Then she catches sight of the living room.

"*Oh...*"

Late yesterday evening, Dad and me hung streamers from the ceiling and blew up balloons until we were red in the face. Rayleen's set the table for six people, with birthday napkins and candles.

"Is this for me?" Prinny says. "Because it's my birthday?" She has tears in her eyes, but they're happy tears.

"You don't have to cook supper tonight," I say. "Your dad's coming here for supper."

"I'm the cook," Rayleen says, wiping her hands on her apron and smiling at Prinny, even though her mother's a Quinn. "You're outta the kitchen tonight, my girl."

Hector arrives ten minutes later with a package under his arm, and the three of us go see Blackie and the kittens. Felix is in the back room because of the party, but mostly he's been loose in the house when Dad and me are home. He's okay with us, but he's not that happy with strangers yet. And every night he marches off to his box to sleep.

Around five-thirty, Dad gets home. His present's done up with a fancy bow. When Prinny's dad arrives in his overalls and a clean T-shirt, Dad pours him a beer and they start talking.

Rayleen says, "Supper's ready," so we all go to the table. The roast chicken's great. Then Rayleen turns out the lights and brings in a cake with twelve candles on it, and we all sing "Happy Birthday."

Prinny's cheeks are pink. She unwraps her presents, *oohing* and *aahing* over smelly hand cream, a new scarf and mittens, a fleece vest from Dad, and a recipe book from Rayleen. Last of all, I give her a card. It has two kittens on the front; inside, it says Blackie's kittens are moving to her place once they're old enough.

She reads it once, then reads it again. "Did I get this right?" she says. "Da? Can I really have the kittens?"

"Long as you looks after them."

"Oh, I will," she says. "I will! *Two* kittens—but shouldn't Hector get one?"

We explain about Hector and Blackie. "You can come and visit the kittens anytime," she says to me and Hector, her eyes shining because there's tears in them again. "I gotta come up with names. Just think—two kittens!"

Because it's a school night, the party breaks up early. Before Prinny goes out the door, she says, "That was the best birthday I ever had. Thanks, Travis."

Then Dad and me wash the dishes. Lots and lots of dishes.

I do my homework, say good night, and go to bed. For a while I lie awake, staring at the ceiling, too full of chocolate fudge icing and too pumped by the birthday party to sleep.

I'm not finished with Gulley Cove. Patches is still on the loose out there; Dr. Larkin gave us an extra trap this morning, and I'll stop putting food in the fourth shack, so that should help. I need to spend more time at Abe's, too, trying to tame the other cats.

Hud's a big question mark. I've got the feeling he could backslide easy.

Then there's the experiment. I don't know how I feel about St. John's anymore. Now that Dad and me are straightened away, where we live doesn't seem to matter as much. I still miss Grady, but not near as bad as I did in October. Maybe we'll always be friends, no matter where we live.

Prinny and Hector are my friends, for sure. From Hector I'm going to learn how to hammer a nail and not my thumb; and from Prinny, how to walk the barrens like I'm a caribou. Abe's my friend, too, and Lucy. Plus Buck, Stevie, Cole, and me are working on setting up plays at hockey. We'll billet together at the first tournament in Port Saunders.

Then, *zonk*, I must have fallen asleep.

When I wake up, it's the middle of the night. There's a big weight on top of me, and this weird noise, like a snowmobile revving up in the distance. For a moment I panic, thinking it's Hud.

I lie still, waiting for my eyes to work in the dark.

The weight is Felix, curled up on my chest.

He's purring.

Author's Note

I write alone, beginning in the wrong place, ending at what often isn't the ending. A big pile of paper, that's the aim. And then come the revisions, which is where my thanks—rightly—begin.

With great gratitude, I salute:

The Gang and the Abbey Girls, including Sister Kate, for their constant presence.

Budge Wilson, who generously shared her wisdom about writing and publication.

Norene Smiley, for editorial insights that caused me to tear the book apart, rearrange, and rewrite.

Mary Jo Anderson, Sue MacLeod, Don Sedgwick, and Lynn Bennett, whose thoughts and suggestions further shaped the book.

Shari Siamon, my mentor at the Humber College Writing for Young Readers Workshop, who sent me in search of the real ending.

Barbara Markovits, who edged me toward the title.

Dr. Emma Raghavan, of Vetcetera Animal Hospital, for her advice concerning feral cats, feline leukemia, etcetera. Any veterinary errors are my own.

Jane Buss and Susan Mersereau of the Writers' Federation of Nova Scotia, for encouragement and practical guidance.

Charlotte Empey, at Humber's School of Creative and Performing Arts, for establishing the Joseph and Dorothy Walmsley Award in memory of her parents. *The Nine Lives of Travis Keating*, in manuscript form, won the inaugural award at Humber College in 2006.

Josh Bartlett and his father, Brian, who read the book together and told me they loved it—this, during one of those times when I was wondering why anyone ever writes anything. Special thanks, Josh, for sneaking the manuscript under the covers with a flashlight because you wanted to know what happened next.

Karen Bartlett for introducing (or reintroducing) me to the delightful world of children's literature.

My editor, Ann Featherstone, for wanting this book to be the best it can possibly be, and for enlivening the editing process with humor, insight, and the fruits of experience.

My publisher, Gail Winskill: she's the reason you're reading this. Thank you, Gail!

My son and daughter-in-law, Colin and Dodie MacLean, for answering questions about anything from the five-hole to hanging out the wash.

And finally, my grandson, Stuart MacLean. Without you, Stuart, it would never have occurred to me that Travis's story was waiting to be told. Or Prinny's. Or—who knows?—Hud's.

A portion of the royalties earned from this book will go to the Society for the Prevention of Cruelty to Animals, in appreciation for the vital role they play in protecting abandoned and mistreated animals.